P

Violet & Claire

"The girls save each other, a victory for sweetness. . . ."
— *Los Angeles Times*

"Block sets herself new challenges and meets them with consummate grace in this resonant novel. Her writing is as lush and luminous, as hip and wise as ever. (Starred review) — *Publishers Weekly*

"Like *Weetzie Bat*, *Violet & Claire* captures the passionate nature of teenage friendship; her conversational style is easy to read; and the quirky characters are likable."
— *Jane*

"As always, Block excels in depicting strong and supportive friendships between teen girls. *Violet & Claire* is at its best when the two protagonists reach past their own pain to help each other." — ALA *Booklist*

"Fans of the author's previous works will take to this one; newcomers will be captured by the rainbow iridescence of Block's prose and her hallucinatory descriptions of the darkest of teen angst and shiniest of Hollywood glitz. — *Kirkus Reviews*

Violet & Claire

Francesca Lia Block

JOANNA COTLER BOOKS
An Imprint of HarperCollins*Publishers*

The quotations on pages 127 and 128 are from the song "Bells for Her."
Courtesy of the author and composer, Tori Amos.
Reprinted by permission of Sword and Stone Publishing Inc.

Violet & Claire

Library of Congress Cataloging-in-Publication Data
Block, Francesca Lia.
    Violet & Claire / Francesca Lia Block
        p.   cm.
    "Joanna Cotler books."
    Summary: In search of material for a screenplay they are developing, seventeen-
year-old Violet and her new friend Claire try to make life a movie as they chase
their dreams through dangerously beautiful Los Angeles.
    ISBN 0-06-027749-1. — ISBN 0-06-027750-5 (lib. bdg.)
    ISBN 0-06-447253-1 (pbk.)
    [1. Friendship—Fiction.   2. Authorship—Fiction.   3. Motion pictures—Fiction.
4. Los Angeles (Calif.)—Fiction.]   I. Title.   II. Title: Violet and Claire.
PZ7.B61945Vi   1999   99-23890
[Fic]—dc21   CIP

Typography by Alicia Mikles
❖
First paperback edition, 2000

For Gilda

Violet

❧

The helicopter circles whirring in a sky the color of laundered-to-the-perfect-fade jeans. Clouds like the wigs of starlets—fluffy platinum spun floss. Below, the hills are covered with houses from every place and time—English Tudor manors, Swiss chalets, Spanish villas, California Craftsman. Flowers threaten to grow over their doors and windows like what happened to Sleeping Beauty's castle. Pools flash like jewels in backyards where Sleeping Beauties in sunglasses float topless, waking to sip from goblets of exotica decorated with pineapples, cherries and hibiscus blossoms. On the roads that run between the hills are shiny cars, hard-candy-colored and filled with music.

This is how my movie begins. The credits floating in the pools, written on the license plates, on billboards, lighting up in neon over the bars. I am in the helicopter dressed in Gautier black and shades, pointing out the shots to the cameraman.

3

This is how my movie begins but not my life. My life started seventeen years ago in a hospital in West L.A. There were no cameras at the event, no sign above the hospital announcing the opening of THE LIFE OF VIOLET SAMMS. Maybe there should have been. Who knows, if I got famous, I told myself, it could be very valuable to have all that on film.

I knew even then that I was destined for a life of cinema. It seemed more real to me than real life, sometimes. As soon as I could walk I discovered cable and began to watch the classics. The parents could not get me away from the screen. The first word I learned was "Rosebud." I imitated Ginger Rogers and Fred Astaire, waltzing around the living room. I tried walking like Charlie Chaplin. When Marilyn was on I didn't do anything. I just sat there with my hands stretched out trying to touch her. Why was she just electric static? I thought she'd be as warm and silky as she looked.

Now you might assume that I wanted to be an actress. But that wasn't it at all. That would have limited me. I could never have dreamed of just playing one part, saying somebody else's words, doing what they told me to do like a lovely puppet. No—I wanted to be the one to give the words, and actions, too. I started by directing my dolls, but they did not cooperate. They had none of the vivid but ephemeral essence that emanates from a real star. I could dress them certain ways and twist their bodies around into the right positions, but I was frustrated by the lack of life in their eyes. That was when I began fantasizing about real actors. The boys and girls in the neighborhood never lived up to my expectations. They got bored fast and went off to play games that I never understood. Also, they had an aversion to some of the more strenuous poses that my dolls, with all their lack of emoting ability, always complied with. Speaking of emoting—the neighborhood children weren't much better than my dolls with that. And then, most humiliating of all, *they* rejected *me*! They plotted ways to avoid me after school. I grew up alone but in the best company.

Dating Cary Grant and Bogey at the revival house, hanging with Jarmusch at the art house, spending the night with Garbo and Veronica Lake on my VCR. Wondering why I couldn't find my own little Marilyn and Jimmy Dean to work with. I knew I was worthy of their talents, even then.

And one day, finally, I saw her.

`EXT. HIGH SCHOOL QUAD: DAY`

She was wearing a Tinker Bell T-shirt and her hair was up on her head in a goofy blond ponytail. You could tell she had no idea she was pretty. But I knew that on film she would glow with that weird light that certain people have. I've got an eye for those things.

I was working on my laptop, still trying to figure out what the script was going to be about. Of course it was going to be about me, but even I couldn't take one hundred and twenty minutes of pure Violet. We needed something. We needed a story. The proverbial "we," because so far the only one on the team was me.

There was no one at school that even had a clue what I was up to. They thought I was from another planet, and maybe I am. At least they usually left me alone. The girls admired my clothes and my hair and the boys checked out my body, but none of them wanted to talk to me. They thought I was some heavily attitude-endowed bitch whose only friend was her PowerBook.

Well, it was true. I didn't have many friends. Make that any. And that would have been all right as long as I could have been making movies. But for movies you need to collaborate. It is one of the laws of film, even if you are a dictator. And so, even if I didn't need any friends, I needed an actress. And there she was, sitting under the big magnolia tree with its fat white flowers, her hair up on her head in a ponytail and her scruffy Tinker Bell T-shirt and her toes poking through the holes in her Vans. It took an expert eye to recognize it in her but I recognized it—she was my star, my Miss Monroe junior, my teen queen extraordinaire, my young diva, my sweet celluloid goddess waiting to be captured on the luminous screen.

I was getting ready to talk to her when this boy Steve decided to come over. Atrocious sense of timing—he could never do stand-up, let alone be a leading man. Also, he desperately needed a stylist. I tried to ignore him, but he stood there, insistent, trying to see what I was writing.

"You must have the longest diary of any girl at this school. Is it about all your hot dates?"

I shouldn't have indulged him but I said it wasn't a diary.

"Oh, excuse me. Zine."

He was trying desperately to find some hepcat credentials to whip out. It made me nauseous.

"No, it's not a zine," I said patiently. "It's a screenplay."

"Awesome!" he exclaimed. "Can I read it?"

I bet you can guess my answer, even in the short time we've been acquainted. Unfortunately, he was not so astute. He seemed surprised and said, "If you don't ever do anything except write you'll need Prozac."

This was especially not funny since in junior high I had gained notoriety from a serious bout with depression that caused me to cut my arms with razor blades. I asked him point-blank what it was that he wanted.

Actually, I was kind of surprised when he asked me to the game on Saturday. I never attended high school events. Not that I didn't like sports. I planned someday to have courtside seats at all Sparks games.

Honestly, though, I might have said yes to him. Just for the experience, you know. Something to write about. I mean, no one had really asked me out like that before, to tell you the truth. They were too scared by my shoes or scars or something. It was always about the backseats of cars, that type of thing. But I didn't think I could actually go through with a real date. Where would it lead? And besides, just at that moment I noticed that Miss Tinker Bell was looking really upset. I closed my laptop and said no, thanks.

"Oh, I forgot," he jeered (jeered is an odd word but the only one that fit his taunting tone). "You're way too sophisticated for something as totally high school as a football game."

I excused myself and started to get up. He mimicked me, tossing imaginary hair and putting a hand on his hip. Even if he was auditioning for the role of the high school asshole he wouldn't have gotten the part, believe me. No talent whatsoever. But I had other things to consider. Tinker Bell was really tweaking.

"You okay, Tink?" I asked.

The kids who had formed a circle around her scattered at the sight of me. Was I the wicked witch or something? It always amazed me the effect I had on people.

Tinker Bell, however, did not seem at all distressed by my appearance. She nodded. Up close she seemed even smaller and very thin—she had the body of a twelve-year-old, practically.

I told her I liked her T-shirt and she grinned. Great

teeth, too. Teeth can be very important when they are blown up to the size of Michael Jordan on the screen.

I would have remembered those teeth if I had seen them before. I asked if she was new to our lovely local prison.

She was.

"Why were they harassing you?" I asked, still trying to get her to talk. Her voice would be an important consideration, and so far it didn't seem like she had one.

In fact, she didn't answer again, just shrugged. That was when I noticed the iridescent gauze and wire fairy wings glued onto the back of her shirt. She didn't seem to know (or care) that at this school you couldn't get away with that. But obviously she was an original.

"I'm going to make this movie," I said. "I wonder if you'd be in it."

I was taking a risk, not having heard her voice, but I was so impressed with the wings that I really had to just go for it.

Unfortunately, Tinker Bell got up and started to walk away. I followed her.

"I'm serious," I said.

She stopped and looked down at her feet. The wings were glistening with glitter behind her. "I can't even answer a question out loud in English, and that's my best subject."

Her voice was almost inaudible. But I didn't care. She definitely had something. To make her feel better, I said, "It's a silent movie. Well, mostly. I think." And I figured maybe it would be. I mean, the real masterpieces didn't need words to convey story or emotion. It would force me to pursue the perfect potent image at all times. And what else was filmmaking about if not a series of perfect and potent images strung together like the words of a poem?

Tinker Bell shrugged. Suddenly a sandwich flew past just grazing her ear. It landed with a mayo-soaked slap on the pavement. There was only one thing to do—I picked it up and slammed it back where it came from. I have to admit I was not only defending my future leading lady. Because of my close proximity to her I was suddenly rendered no longer immune. That sandwich could very well have been intended for my own stoned-on-cinema head.

Tinker Bell and I cut class and walked home together. She seemed somewhat overwhelmed by the 'hood—her eyes widening at each house we passed. I was so used to the decadence, it was pathetic. I appreciated her sense of wonder. The large manors with their stone walls and gabled roofs, their emerald lawns and bursts of flowers had been the backdrop of my life for as long as I could remember. But as impressed as she was with it all, Tinker Bell was not taken aback. She blithely collected blossoms from each garden and stuck them in her hair or her backpack.

I was trying to explain to her some of the basic principles of film. It was a relief to at last have someone who would listen, although she seemed more interested in the configurations of flower petals than in my theories.

"The main thing is conflict," I told her.

She paused to jam a blue hydrangea into her backpack. "I don't like conflict," she said. "I'm a Libra."

You know: scales, balancing . . .

I was impressed with her strong opinion, at least, even if this was a huge point of contention. I decided to approach the subject in a semi-circuitous fashion like any good teacher.

"What movies do you like?" I inquired.

"I liked that one with the pig," she said.

"But why did you like it?"

"He was so cute. It reminded me of *Charlotte's Web*."

"But the reason you liked him was because he was in danger," I patiently explained. "I mean, that's what made you really care."

She thought about this for a moment, screwing up her face. I was impressed by her lack of regard for the possibility of wrinkles. I had been raised by a wrinkle-free-fanatic who never smiled or expressed any other emotion as a means to avoid the dreaded lines.

"I guess," she said. "I wouldn't have minded just watching him be a cute pig."

"Well, there's got to be conflict or it's not real film," I preached. I admit I preach in this area. But how can I help it? It is my religion. My only source of faith and fervor.

Tinker Bell's religion was obviously of a different nature. "I like to write poetry," she said. "Poetry doesn't depend on conflict."

We had gotten to my house at this point, and I led her through the spiked fortress of gates and up the path. "You can't make a living from poetry," I told her.

She stared at the white colonial monster in which I had been raised, with its towering, gleaming columns, and she seemed puzzled that I was thinking about making a living.

"This is your house?" she said.

I knew what she was getting at. A rich child like

me should be able to think freely about my future. I should be a purist, a patron of the finer arts. But she didn't understand. I could not ride on my parents coattails (or in their Beemer) for much longer. I had to get out of there and make a living on my own. It was a hellish environment in spite of its apparent glamor. And, unfortunately, because of the way I'd been raised, they had made me used to luxury. I was a certified high-maintenance gal, and the starving-artist life would never have sufficed, no matter how good it sounded in theory.

But it was hard to explain my woes to someone when they were drifting through rooms papered in shiny flowers, decorated in expensive antiques and crystal, under high sky-lit ceilings and over gleaming marble floors.

I took off my shoes and left them by the door as always. When you grow up on white carpets and with a mother like Judy, it's just something you get used to. Tinker Bell slipped off her Vans and followed me past the couches covered in plastic.

She raised her face to the crystal chandelier. Sunlight on the trembling pendants scattered a myriad of rainbows across her face. She blew a bubble with her gum. The thin pink sugar would have looked as good on film as any jewel.

Then she was in my room, up the winding white staircase, in my room and spinning spinning like a 1960's sitcom career girl (think marlo, mary, diane) taking in the decor.

My room seemed like a different planet from the rest of the house. First of all, I am entirely anti-pastel. It comes from growing up amidst daffodil damask couches and sky-blue velvet chairs (plastic-covered, of course), in a room painted Pepto Bismol. So, what was a pastel-saturated young thing to do? My obsession with black had started very young. My hair was dyed jet. My closet contained angora sweaters low-slung hiphuggers micro minis tummy baring midriffs fluffy chubbies platforms stilettos and sandals in black black black. Only black. Obsidian. My prize possession—the 1965 'Stang—was, of course, pure ebony. Therefore,

17

the theme applied to my environment as well. I had painted over the Abysmal Pink with black paint when I was twelve (all on my own, mind you, I was a rich child but industrious). The only decor was my *film noir* posters, my film theory books and the 3x5 index cards tacked up alongside my storyboards.

As was my daily custom after school, I went up to the wall and began to rearrange the cards. I had started to do it randomly to see the surrealist possibilities and break the conventions of plot point and arc. Of course, this was merely theoretical. As rebellious as I was, I knew the importance of classic story structure. Unfortunately, there were still large gaps in my story.

"Have you always loved movies?" Tinker Bell asked me, staring at my *Pulp Fiction* poster (the only contemporary non-noir in the room; I was a reluctant Quentin disciple).

I answered her in the affirmative, deciding to spare her the historical details.

"Are your parents writers?" she asked.

It wasn't a bad guess (from their house you could have guessed they wrote cheesy blockbusters or something) but it was as far from the truth as could be. They were—and I told her this—the major bores. "They don't even know who Cocteau is."

"How lame!" Tink exclaimed. And then—it was endearing somehow, coming from her: "Who?"

I said that I could see I needed to educate her. She abruptly plopped down on my (black) floor and took a cardboard star out of her backpack. I continued to maneuver the 3x5's. Currently, the heroine was fighting with her parents in the opening scene.

"How'd you learn all this stuff?" she asked.

"I'm entirely self taught. I rent two videos a night and I read everything."

Tink took a glitter pen and tape out of her backpack.

"What's your movie going to be about?" she asked.

I paused and turned toward her. I had been waiting for this moment for a long time: when someone who was not a thorough dweebish boll weevil would ask me about my project. Even though I still didn't really know what it was going to be about, I knew certain things for certain. "It's going to be terrifically cool. It's going to be really dark but with this kind of glowing color emanating from it."

She began to glitter up the star, then paused, lost in thought.

"Like when you were a kid and you used to make a design with colored crayons and then cover it with black and then scratch it and the color showed through?"

That was pretty good. "Yes," I said. "Like stained glass."

We both stopped and stared reverently into space, seeing the glossy glassy colors, the rose window of a church. As much as I loved black on and around my limbs, I always appreciated the wonder of Technicolor, the possibilities of the palette.

"Cool," Tinker Bell whispered, as if inside a cathedral.

Then she broke the spell with her question. "So, what's the conflict?"

"What?" I said, annoyed by the interruption of my reverie.

"You said the most important thing is . . ."

"That's the problem," I confided to her. "I honestly don't know yet. I don't have any exciting conflict in my life. And you're always supposed to write from experience. It gives authenticity."

At that moment, right on cue—she did have dramatic timing, I'd say that for Judy—we heard my name being called.

"Oh shit," I said.

Tinker Bell reflexively hid her star.

"Is that you?" Judy said, opening the door that I had forgotten to lock. "You scared me to death!"

"Sorry," I mumbled.

"I thought we were being burglarized."

I repeated that I was sorry and that we'd been let out early. She proceeded to repeat that she had thought I was a burglar and that I should be more careful because one of these times she might get really scared and find my father's gun. As you can see, she is really out of her mind. I used to worry that it might run in the family.

"Who's this?" she asked, sizing up my new friend.

I didn't want to say Tinker Bell, so I was glad that Tink spoke up and told us. "Claire."

It was the right name for her, I thought. Almost as fitting as her nickname.

My mother lost interest in Claire even before she'd said her name. She walked out, complaining about burglars.

"It's like we're not even the same species or something," I said.

"Like Peanuts." Claire fastened her star onto the end of a ruler from her backpack.

What was she talking about?

She explained: the cartoon. "Where the parents are just this waaa-waaa-waaa voice thing."

"That's brilliant," I said. "Can I use it?"

She nodded. I made a note on my tape recorder:

"Parents. Waaa-waaa-waaa voice thing. Peanuts."

Claire touched her star wand to the top of my head and grinned like a slightly deranged young fairy godmother.

The thing that was so frustrating about my parents the Waaa-waaas was that they didn't even give me the standard sitcom parent/teen conflict, let alone high drama. It was so boring. (Well, the line about the gun wasn't totally without merit). Not that I envied children who had been abused, but I had to admit that sometimes I wanted something more, something to explain why I felt so alienated and depressed, except for the times I was living inside the movies. My parents knew nothing about me. They had no interest in cinema. I really did feel as if I was someone else's child. Maybe the great Italian genius director, Federico Fellini, and his brilliant muse/collaborator/wife, Giulietta Masina, had had a secret baby and, sensing her truculent nature, put her in a tiny boat sailing to America. Maybe someone had found her on the shore and taken her to an orphanage where a rich couple had adopted her. Then, when they brought her home, they realized she was not what they wanted at all. She did not like pastels. She liked only black. She did not make friends with the other children. She began to develop earlier than the other girls. She cut herself with razor blades just to see her own blood. Only the movies saved her, but the Waaa-waaas couldn't understand this. It was as if they spoke another language. Waaa-waaa-waaa.

All this would have made fairly interesting material for my script, but not scintillating. And I wanted scintillating. I wanted to scintillate, titillate, mesmerize, hypnotize. I needed, in short, an adventure to remove my writer's block.

When I told Claire about it at school the next day she said, "Maybe we could go hiking or something."

"An urban adventure," I explained. I had to get out into the world. The high school *Fast Times at Ridgemont High* comedy had had its day. Even *Clueless,* although I had to admit I agreed with

Claire about finding Alicia rather sweet in it. But the world was looking for more action. Tarentinoesque. A kind of female *Pulp Fiction* but with more soul.

When I told that to Claire she pretended to stab her chest, a la Uma in the *Pulp.* "I hated that scene with the . . ." she said.

It wasn't a bad impression. "I knew you'd be a good actress," I told her.

Just then Steve slogged over. Slogged because of those big pants.

"How's the *movie* going, Violet?" he asked prickishly.

I answered politely.

"Is that your new leading lady?"

We ignored him.

"She looks just like Sharon Stone. Especially the hair."

"And you're Johnny Depp, aren't you?" was my retort.

I guess someone had been helping Steve with his dialogue because he came back with, "I could look

25

like him and you still wouldn't go out with me. I didn't know you liked girls."

I closed my laptop and we started to leave.

"I knew it. Dykes."

Claire said, "What's your problem? Why are you so mean?"

"Why are you so rank?" was Steve's clever response.

I told him to fuck off. He said, "Fuck me."

We walked away. Claire told me that I should just ignore him.

"He's an asshole," I said. "But he just gave me some great material."

When you look at pain as material it makes all the difference in the world. I thought, the pain that is too big to be eased by its use as material would be a pain I couldn't (and wouldn't want to) even imagine.

EXT. CLAIRE'S HOUSE: NIGHT

Claire and her mother were living in a small stucco bungalow behind a jungle of bamboo and banana trees. I honked the horn and she came racing out with her ponytail bopping around on her head. She was wearing a polka-dot thrift shop dress.

I used to come to the silent movie theater on Fairfax all the time when I was a kid. Once I ran away from home and tried to live there, but the manager caught me and called the authorities.

Claire stood in front of the black-and-white mural of Charlie, Buster and Mary Pickford with their deep sad eyes. She did a little imitation of the Tramp. It wasn't bad. I got the tickets for us and she tried to pay me, but I could tell she was grateful when I wouldn't accept. Also, she said she didn't want anything from the concession stand, but I got an extra-large Diet Coke and popcorn anyway, and she asked for two straws and for them to put extra butter on the popcorn.

The thing about silent films, Claire had told me, is that she couldn't help talking during them and she hoped I didn't mind. I'd seen *City Lights* so often that I figured it would be okay, although usually

I didn't like to be disturbed while contemplating, deconstructing and exploring the semiotics of a piece.

"Well, at least the talk with your parents will make a good scene," Claire said when she had gotten me to reveal, after a lot of prodding, what was pissing me off so much. The Waaa-waaas were refusing to send me to film school. They thought I should attend a regular college and go into law.

"It'll make a sucky scene," I said. "That's not feature-quality drama. It's *90210* at best."

"You could put fairies in the movie," she said.

I turned to look at her. What?

"Fairies," she said again, "you know."

She said it too loud and the couple of guys next to us leaned over and glared. They obviously thought it was a personal dis of some kind.

"That's not radical enough anymore," I informed her. "I mean, that's prime time now. That's *Melrose Place.*"

"I mean the real fairies," she insisted, making

delicate flapping motions with her arms. She really was on this Tinker Bell kick for some reason.

"The *real* fairies?" Yeah right. "What is a real fairy? That sounds *very* intense."

I realized then that Miss Claire was serious about this stuff.

"Actually, it is, Violet." (She was miffed.) "Faeries—and that's a-e-r-i-e, not a-i-r-y—were a race of people who were exterminated. Just like they tried to do in Germany. They were incredibly powerful. The patriarchy turned them into little insects."

Her eyes took on a cricket-green glow in the darkness. "That's pretty cool," I had to admit.

The gentlemen beside us had a different opinion. They must have been offended by the fairy thing. Make that faerie.

"Could you please *shutup*," one of them hissed.

Claire realized the misunderstanding and started to turn around to explain it to them, but I grabbed her wrist.

When the movie was over we walked outside, and I told her about how I had run away when I was little, about coming to the theater and wanting to move in there.

"I figured I could hide out in the bathrooms until they closed and then sneak out and live on popcorn and candy for the rest of my life. Get to know those movies by heart, too."

I took a long drag on my cigarette and imagined the smoke turning into winged creatures.

"That sounds fun," she said. "Maybe you could write about a faerie who's caught in this world and she doesn't belong. It's so corrupt and all ugly and she wants to be this true-love thing. So she runs away and lives in a movie theatre."

It wasn't bad but it lacked something. "I need more conflict," I said.

At that moment we came to a ladder, which I blithely cruised under. Claire pulled me away.

"I wish you'd stop saying that. It seems like bad luck or something."

As she spoke a black cat jumped down onto the ladder, knocking a can of paint off a rung. The red paint splattered down in the place where I would have been standing if she hadn't grabbed me. I wondered if Claire was my good luck charm, somehow. I felt fearless.

"Let's have an adventure!" I said.

When I was thirteen I went through this whole Goth phase. Death rock. Skulls and crossbones. That's when I first dyed my hair black, although it was much shorter than it is now, and started smoking cigarettes. I called myself Vile. That was when I cut my arms with a razor blade as a means of creative expression. I only did it lightly, just grazing the skin, to see the way the blood would bleed out, to make myself look tougher. Not like some of those kids who keep going deeper and deeper, wondering what they look like down to the bone, because it's a world that's so close and yet so far and so dangerous and so much their own. The only world that is their own. I wasn't that gone. But it did get pretty bad. The worst part was when things started to blur and stir in my head and I thought I might be becoming like Judy. I thought there were men trying to get in the house or watching me when I walked to school. I had headaches and trouble breathing, and once I got sent home for talking to myself in homeroom; I don't remember it, though.

Movies literally saved my life then. I had briefly entertained the notion of becoming president when I grew up. This was in sixth grade. I wanted to change the world. I was disgusted by what I saw on the news, but not defeated by it. I believed in myself.

It's weird what happens to girls at a certain point in their lives. One moment they're these tough little things, racing around, jabbering, excited about just waking up to see what else is new in the world. Everything just opening for them, it seems like. That was how I felt. And then suddenly I was Vile. I hated everyone. I never spoke in class. I gave up wanting to be president.

Actually, I wanted to die. It came right around when I had my first period. No one explained to me about PMS or anything. My mother gave me Midol for the cramps and said, "Congratulations, welcome to the Curse." Once she got mad at me for not wrapping up my used tampons carefully enough when I threw them in the garbage. Vile, you see.

That was when I started smoking and stopped talking and just changed completely. That was when the only thing that soothed me was the movies. I began to believe in them more than in the world. Now Claire made me feel the way they did.

I hit PLAY, and the PJ Harvey CD started up. Claire and I jolting with music as we drive through the air that was so sweet with jasmine and honeysuckle it could have been golden or silver.

I didn't feel afraid of anything. I felt like when I was twelve years old. I had this best friend, Mandy Appleman. She was a real character. She thought I was the cat's p.j.s. "You're going to be the next Antonioni,

Violet," she'd say. "Unless of course you decide to be president." We wore boys' boxer shorts and insisted we would never shave our legs when we got older. We made huge batches of cookie dough, half of which we consumed raw, the other half of which we baked and then gorged upon. We discovered old punk rock albums from the eighties and played them as loud as possible, slamming around my room until we collapsed with exhaustion, having burned off all the cookie dough. She was even skinnier than I was. We were proud of our boyish bodies, our flat chests. It was like we had wheels on our feet and psychic antennae for each other. Supernatural rolling girl aliens. Until she moved to New York. I was devastated, I exaggerate not. Suddenly I was in junior high, I was Vile, I was smoking cigarettes every day. Really, since Mandy Appleman I hadn't even had any friends. I had breasts which gave me power and made me endangered simultaneously. I had no friends. Until Claire. My insta-friend. Claire made me feel brave.

With PJ still wailing and the air still glinting with

fragrance, we drove to the Red Cherry, which was this transvestite bar in Hollywood that I'd always wanted to check out. A red neon cherry was flashing on and off inside a neon cocktail glass over the door. I donned my shades and lit a cigarette before we went in. Claire looked a little nervous. I reassured her that our fake i.d.s (I'd gotten her one, too) would work.

The girls in the Red Cherry were tremendous. Emerging from clouds of red smoke, they looked like superfreak goddesses with the longest legs and manes of synthetic hair. I was just wondering if any of them would be interested in sharing their stories with us when ESMERALDA (here I want to capitalize her name as in a film script—it was that kind of entrance, very dramatic) rolled up to us in her wheelchair. Her makeup looked like cake frosting applied with a spatula, and she wore a cherry-red bubble wig. Her emaciated, twisted body was sheathed in a revealing black cocktail dress and there were spike heels on her gnarled feet.

"Hello, ladies," Esmeralda intoned, in a voice that

was both growling and shrill, somehow.

I said hello and she asked, "What, pray tell, are you doing at La Maraschino?"

I tried not to miss a beat. "We're going to be making a movie."

Esmeralda's eyes lit up like neon cherries. "Oh really! Well I'll have you know that you are speaking to a full-fledged film star. Really! I've done everything! I'm brilliant if I do say so myself."

"I think you'd be perfect for my film," I assured her. You didn't find a girl like her around everyday. I thought about Claire's faerie theory. Esmeralda could have easily been part of some other race, banished underground and now emerging in disguise to reclaim her birth rite.

"Bless your heart," she said, extending one gnarled and perfectly manicured hand adorned with a serious rock. "Want to see my wedding ring?"

Claire took the hand gently in her own and examined the ring. "That's pretty."

Esmeralda batted the false eyelashes that looked

so heavy I wondered how she kept her eyes open under their weight.

"Thank you, sweetheart. I'm engaged to a man named Elvis. He's a real hound dog. What's your movie going to be about?"

"We're not sure yet," said Claire.

I gave her a look, but she didn't seem to get it. I realized that I'd have to make sure she didn't talk about the project too much without my coaching.

"Sounds fascinating!" Esmeralda said with a growling but somehow shrill snort. "Why don't you make it be about this absolutely stunning young lady who once had a very silly willy wonka. A very bothersome diddley dee. But then she meets this dashing gentleman and he finances the operation and presto! No more flippery flap!"

We were both trying to take this all in when MATILDA (I cannot resist the caps), a hugely muscled six foot tall bleach blond African American trans, slunk over on sinewy espresso legs in shimmery sheer cream stockings.

Esmeralda introduced her to us and Matilda said, "Girlfriend, are you saying shocking things to these ladies?"

"She's very interesting," I assured Matilda. "We're making a movie."

"Really?" Matilda's primping was an automatic reaction to this. She was, after all, a Hollywood girl. "What's it about?"

Before Claire could spoil things I told her. "Well, it's going to be kind of an allegory utilizing very poetic imagery but with a gritty edge of realism."

Esmeralda and Matilda frowned. "Hmmm," Matilda hummed. "Why not make something about us! We're very popular in Hollywood these days. They made like *two* movies about girls with the very same plot! And one of them had big stars in it."

Esmeralda looked as if she were going to spit. "You would have been better than that one actor, though!" she exclaimed. "I mean, who would ever cast *him*? No style, whatsoever. Like a football player on Halloweenie."

Claire was cracking up, but I tried to be professional. "Well if I were going to make a movie about girls like you I'd cast girls like you," I assured them.

Matilda grinned at me. "Would you ladies care for a drink? We can discuss the biz."

I could see Claire hesitating, about to excuse us, so I elbowed her (adventure!) and told Matilda we'd be delighted.

After a few drinks we were dancing like maniacs with Esmeralda and Matilda. Claire had loosened up and was pushing Esmeralda's wheelchair around and around a man whom we will call ELVIS (definite caps) here. Esmeralda blew him kisses as she passed, which he deftly caught and inserted into the breast of his blue and silver spangled suit.

"Love interest!" Esmeralda shouted as Claire spun her around me.

"What?"

"You need a love interest," she hollered above the Donna Summer song. "Every good script has love interest!"

She was right. So did every good life. Therefore, neither my script nor my life would qualify.

I was cheered by the thought that if I found love interest I would most certainly also find the conflict that I was so adamantly pursuing.

Later, as we were about to leave, I overheard Esmeralda talking to Claire. "And what do you do on this film, Missy?"

"Violet wants me to be in it."

"Another actress!" Esmeralda exclaimed.

"Not really." Claire shuffled her feet. I realized we'd have to work on her reply. She added, "What I really like to do is write poetry."

Just perfect! I'd really have to coach her.

"Poetry!" Esmeralda was in rapture at the mere mention of the word. "Poetry is the food of the soul. Would you like to hear some of my poetry? 'The dark withered angel turned prophetic eyes to the horizon. In that flash of cinder and rubble my body was transformed . . .'"

"I think she's a faerie," Claire whispered to me.

Suddenly I was swept up in the glittery arms of Elvis. His black pompadour smelled of Aquanet (familiar from my Goth phase). Shadows and disco lights were playing on his face, giving him an ominous expression, like the real King returned from the dead with tidings.

"Do you like Spent Pleasure?" he asked me.

Was he kidding? "Am I female and under the age of thirty?" I replied. Who didn't love Spent Pleasure, the hottest band of life? Even I, Miss independent loner not-into-what-you're-into, had succumbed many times to the devastating charms of their lead singer, Flint Cassidy. I even harbored a poster of him in the dark depths of my black closet. He was nihilistic yet a romantic, post-postmodern and pure classicism blended into an ageless icon. A demon Eros for our time. I hated to admit it, but Flint Cassidy awakened in me all the desires I so longed to sublimate into film.

"My sources tell me they're playing at the Raunch Room tomorrow night," Elvis said.

"The Raunch Room!" It was a teeny tiny venue. I knew that Flint and his flunkies had sold out the Forum already, which was why I hadn't even attempted to get tickets.

"It's a special top secret gig," Elvis informed me. "And there are plenty of tickets still."

"Oh my God! That's awesome! Thank you!"

But Elvis had something else on his big-haired mind. "Make sure they meet cute."

"What?"

"It's a Hollywood expression. It's when the boy meets the girl in this really cute way. Like she faints, and he's the one who catches her?"

I was so caught up with the idea of seeing Flint Cassidy up close at the Raunch Room (close enough to feel his sweat, close enough to see his nose hairs) that I had forgotten about my movie for once. I didn't know what Elvis was referring to.

"In your script," he said impatiently. He had tiny, sharp teeth. "Make them meet cute."

Meet cute. I wrote a note on the script when I got in that night. Of course, if I was going to employ this concept I'd have to have a love interest. And so far, there wasn't any on the horizon. This point was hammered in painfully when I got to school the next day and looked around. The science nerds—what is that thing with pants pulled up too high and tight and flood-ankles; I just don't get it. It's almost like it goes with the I.Q.—very strange. Surfers—now they look all right with their hair bleached out and their tans, but when you talk to them, it's always this drawl like the sun fried their brains or something. Hippies—I'm sorry, it's just about thirty years too late for peace and love. But they're better than the asshole jocks—they scare me. And why does everybody have to fit into some category? Even generic boys like Steve, they all have to wear those baggy-ass pantaloons and backwards baseball caps and Nikes. Occasionally I'd eye some punk rocker or grungster or techno boy or Mr. Indie, but there weren't too many of them and besides, I was seeking an original with whom to

43

meet cute. An original—and someone over the age of twenty. Otherwise, how could I expect them to share my passion for film noir, cinema verité and dada?

In English class I was trying to work on the script, but Steve was looking over my shoulder, sticking his schnoz in, reminding me further of the lack of potential love interests in my life. He didn't really care about what I was writing; of course it was more about my mini dress and vinyl go-go boots. My teacher, Miss Henderson, did not have such a fondness for my fashion sense; in fact I think she hated it. Plus, she knew I didn't give a shit about her class—I'd read everything three years ago, anyway.

"Violet!" she was saying. "Violet!"

I emerged, startled, from my dream of meeting cute. If Miss Henderson were to appear in my film, she would most certainly be treated as the "Waaa-waaa voice thing" that Claire had conceived of so brilliantly. She was Miss Waaa-waaa voice thing. There was nothing else impressive enough about her to make it to the screen. Film was precious.

But Miss Henderson's voice could stay; she provided the conflict that I needed.

"I'm sorry," I said. "What was the question"

"*Macbeth,* Violet. Your schoolwork?"

"Yes, I read it" (when I was eight). "I just didn't hear the question."

"You need to start paying attention," waaa-waaaed the voice. "Anyone?"

There was a long silence. Finally the Waaa-waaa spoke, and if you did see her face, you would have noticed that she was glaring at me venomously. "Lady Macbeth's fatal flaw was ambition!"

Ambition. Well, sometimes I got something out of school. I typed the word in at lunch that day. Ambition. I wondered, had I been born with it? Where did it come from? Where did Lady MacB's fatal ambition come from? And why did ambition have to be a flaw? Let alone fatal?

While I typed, hawk eyed, the A word on my screen, my innocent counterpart slept peacefully on the bench, recovering from our adventure of the night before, her head resting on my backpack. Her eyelids fluttered pixieishly.

"I'm glad you're resting," I said. "Because we have to go out again tonight."

She opened her eyes and yawned. "Where we going?"

"We definitely need another adventure," I informed her. "We need a love interest. Esmeralda was right. You won't believe who's doing an undercover show at the Raunch Room."

`INT. RAUNCH ROOM: NIGHT`

A sexy, pale-skinned rock god, a post-punk Eros, FLINT CASSIDY, is stalking and flaunting on the stage of a small, packed club. Kids are moshing wildly to his band, Spent Pleasure, trying to touch him. You can almost see the steam rising off of bare skin.

Our heroines stand near the stage, crushed by moshers, transfixed.

(singing)

Girl Jesus you're so thin
Sleep on my cross for your sins
When you ever gonna let me in?
I guess this has to be a kind of redemption

Girl Vampire you're so red
Sleep in a box like you were dead
Just another demon in my head
I wish you'd bite me and then we'd go to bed

Girl Angel you blind my eyes
I sleep on the cloud of your thighs
When you touch me you make me rise
Are you wearing just another disguise

Girl Satan you love me the most
I am your father son and holy ghost
Will you betray me if you can't get close
Or within the circle of your flames I will roast

47

✧ ✧ ✧

Thus came to me a perfect scene for my film. I stood there in my vinyl pants, achieving ecstasy. Perhaps it was less about the dude and more about the void he filled in my project. No matter, I had found my love interest. I only needed one thing—to be able to cutely meet him.

"How did you hear about this?" Claire hollered into my ear, her voice chiming painfully through my head.

I rubbed the sore orifice. "I have my ways," I said.

Suddenly, Flint Cassidy's whole body tensed like a panther and he sprang off the stage into the crowd. It caught and held him like the ocean as he kept singing. And then it happened. His eyes met mine. He was supported just above me. I could have almost reached out and licked the sweat from his face. There was a tantric charge that I had read about but never felt before. It started in my groin and went shooting up my belly, through my heart, my throat, exploding out the top of my head like a burning lotus blossom. I knew that Flint was a natural, the real thing. A constellation, comet, supernova star. His image would burn a hole through the screen when it was projected there.

Using every trick I had ever learned from the lambent orbs of the great goddesses of screen, I kept eye contact with Flint Cassidy as I pulled Claire along behind me toward the backstage door.

I showed the bouncer my screenplay and gave some discourse on the perfect part for Flint, but I have to admit my diatribe did not impress him. He was, however, interested in my pants and corset. Sometimes, in this world of ours, vinyl speaks louder than words. No matter. It worked. Claire and I were admitted into the lair.

And there he was, lying back in a chair wearing only torn black jeans, worn thin at the crotch (!), and thinner at the knees, both of which (the knees) stuck out nakedly; combat boots on his size thirteen feet. He was pouring Jack Daniel's into a bottle of Gatorade and guzzling it down.

There were pretty girls everywhere, but it was to me whom he turned and at me whom he pointed one Flint finger. I was able to *maintain* but of course my dear young Claire was practically levitating with excitement. I noticed Flint whispering something to his bass player, who, like all the band members, resembled a smaller clone of the lead-god.

The bass player swaggered over to us, with that too-tight-pant rock-star walk, and summoned us to meet his leader. I paused to light a cigarette as if contemplating the pros and cons of this proposition. Then, as cooly as if I were approaching the produce section of the supermarket to purchase apples, I followed the bass player over to Flint.

"So, how's it going?" he asked me.

He had a kind of crackling speaking voice.

"It's going great," I crackled back.

"Enjoy the show?" He lit up too and squinted through the smoke at me.

"You have a lot of charisma," I told him. I was not one to give compliments and I suddenly wished I hadn't said it, especially when he didn't reply, just kept staring at me.

"That's a good thing," I said, perhaps a little 'tudey.

He didn't like condescension. "Yes, babe, I know what charisma is, believe me."

"Then why don't you say thank you? I thought you weren't sure if I was giving you a compliment."

My face was getting warm and I prayed I wasn't blushing. I fanned myself with the script.

"What's that?" he asked.

"It's my screenplay," I said, glad to have reconnected with my intention for being here. My power would return if I concentrated on the project, I was sure. It always worked for me. I was surprised I had let myself get so off track.

He asked me what it was about and I replied, "It could be about you if you learn to say thank you when someone compliments you."

"You're a feisty chicky," Flint retorted. "Why don't you and your friend hang out a while and we'll go party later."

I suddenly remembered Claire and felt a pang of guilt. It wasn't a good sign that I had forgotten about my screenplay and my friend after just moments in the presence of Mr. Hotshit Rockstar.

I looked for Tinker Bell and saw her hovering behind me like a sprite bestowing blessings. Moments later we were dancing wildly together. There is nothing so good almost as dancing with a great girl dancer. It seems so much more natural than dancing with some stiff guy who won't look you in the eye. If he's shy he'll watch the walls and if he's an asshole he'll ogle your tits, but a great girlfriend dancer will look at you with the knowledge that between you, you are weaving a magic circle where music and beauty live. She will not be afraid of any expression of power. She will say to you with her eyes, "This is our spell we are casting." That is what Claire and I did. Cool as I try to remain, when I hear a great song, I just go ballistic. I'm jumping off the ground and shaking orgasmically. It was great. Flint thought so, too, I could tell. He watched us the whole time, even when those chicks came to sit on his lap and fondle his obscenely naked knees.

After a while Flint removed the latest girl from his lap and came over to me. I danced around him, trying to seem oblivious, until he seized my hand and pulled me toward him.

"I'm heading back to the hotel. Do you want to come with me and show me your script?"

He had chosen the perfect line. I couldn't think of how to resist. I stopped dancing. Claire did, too; she'd heard him. A big smile twinkled on her face.

"I have to take my friend home," I said.

"I can get my driver to take her if you want."

"That's cool!" Claire reassured me.

I asked her if she was positive. She nodded so that her ponytail bopped around. I kissed her cheek and whispered my gratitude into her ear.

`INT. LIMO: NIGHT`

In Flint's limo I decided, I could live here! It was the perfect apartment with a wet bar and deep plush seats, tiny stars of light studding the ceiling around the moon roof. An endless supply of the best champagne. Flint poured me a glass and we clinked as the car sped down Sunset. Then I asked if I could interview him—for the film, I said, pulling out my tape recorder. He seemed pleased.

"Most people are chickenshit," he intoned when I asked him his philosophy of life. "They're afraid of their own dark natures. But that's what life is about, man. It's about darkness as well as light. If you don't acknowledge the one, you are thoroughly fucked. You will never know the other."

To tell you the truth, I was impressed. In spite of his hipper-than-thou attitude and rock star posturing, the words made a lot of sense to me. In fact, they were words I tried to live by.

"*Carpe noctum!* Seize the night, you know what I mean? Take what you can get. Even if it seems wicked. I mean, what's the alternative? Rot. Death."

I imagined the scene in the movie. Girl cynic gliding through the neon-glossed night in the perfect bachelor pad on wheels while rock god extraordinaire becomes increasingly beautiful in the motion-and-champagne-charged atmosphere. By the time we arrived at the hotel I had fully succumbed. There is a strange thing about certain celebrities—a heat or radiance that magnetizes. All you want is to be close to them. And that wasn't like me. But it was as if I might be able to absorb some of his power. I wondered where it resided in him. There was a luster to his eyes and hair and a depth to his musculature that was seeming more and more supernatural. I was, however, just doing research. Love interest and all that.

But later, when he had me on the vast golden bed in the hotel room and was unleashing my breasts from the vinyl corset, I forgot the movie entirely. Around us the room spun—a merry-go-round of champagne bottles, champagne grapes on silver platters, boxes of chocolates, arrangements of flowers like small trees. The sheets were stiff starched white cool linen and Flint's skin was sleek and warm. I was surprised by the freckles on his shoulders. I pressed my head to his chest and heard the watery thud of his heart.

Still, I am not a complete fool. When he was hard against me I reached for my purse, without missing a kissing beat, and felt around for the small crispy packet.

"Use this."

Flint pushed my hand away.

"It's not my size," he said, without even looking (what did he think he was, extra-large jumbo or something?).

"I am so serious, use it or get the fuck off me," was my reply. Unsafe sex is one thing I was not going to mess around with.

This comment must have surprised him, because he stopped and looked at me for the first time. We both had the same determined pissed-off expression on our faces, and then his shifted, softened somehow and he just said, "You remind me of me, Violet."

Once in a while a good line comes to me spur-of-the-moment, out-of-the-blue. Maybe good enough for the script, although I must admit at the time I was not thinking about art.

"No I don't," I told him. "I have a much bigger supply of condoms than you do."

Not only did it sound all right but it worked well, too, because he took the rubber then.

Sex is such the weird thing. I mean, I love it, actually, but I decided a few years ago that I'd try to be circumspect. I was born a sensuality addict; anything that stimulates my senses pleasurably is enough for me to do heroic deeds to obtain, and sex combined all senses at once when it was good. Or at least I imagined it *could* combine them all at once though I had to admit I hadn't had the experience I was seeking yet. With Flint it came kind of close. He seemed to know my body so well; probably because he'd been with so many others, but still. He whispered my name in my ear like an incantation; I was glad he even *remembered* it after all the drugs he'd probably consumed. His tongue probed the ridges on the roof

57

of my mouth and his teeth gently bit at my lips. I was balanced above him like flying, held by my hipbones in his palms, my hair and his blending together black and shiny on the feathery pillows, our mouths exchanging silent secrets. That was the way I liked to think of it, anyway. That's how it would be in my movie.

And then afterward we were smoking and eating expensive chocolates and he was flipping through the script and I was trying to be cool but thinking, Flint Cassidy is holding my movie in his hands.

"You're pretty young to be such a serious writer," Flint said, narrowing his eyes at me over the pages.

"I used to be into politics when I was little," I told him. "I wanted to be president and change the world, end injustice and everything. But then I hit puberty and it seemed too difficult. I decided I'd try to change the world through art. And film reaches a lot of people."

Flint stopped mid-chocolate to listen. When I was done he swallowed and said, "I told you you reminded me of me."

That was when I knew I had to get out of there. Fast. But by trying to escape the feelings of vulnerability I made it worse; I was naked in front of him, sinking into the deep soft carpet, woozy on the smell of the flowers. To hide myself I grabbed the first thing I could reach—his leather jacket with "Spent Pleasure" painted on the back—and held it in front of me as I backed toward the bathroom.

"Where you going? Come back here."

It was the desired response but not to be responded to in the affirmative. "I have work to do," I said.

"You are serious. Can I see you again?"

Someone was doing an admirable job with Flint's script. I'd have hired them.

"Maybe," I told him.

"I'll give you my address," he said, and I hurried (backward because of my state of undress) into the bathroom so he wouldn't see the childish glee that was about to hop onto my face like an army of imps.

I felt that there was something momentous

about my meeting with Flint Cassidy. However, my perceptions were skewed. Yes, momentous—I could trace back to him the series of events that eventually changed my life. But I had thought Flint might change my life a different way. It felt sick to admit it, even to my trusted Tinker Claire, but when I was with him I didn't care so much about completing or selling my script or making the movie. It was the first time I had ever felt that way. Instead, I began to fantasize about being a devoted wife. Rather sick, but true. I saw the ornate Victorian mansion in New Orleans with the recording studio in the basement where I would reign, floating down the mahogany staircase in a long black gown to greet our guests; my husband, that untamed panther no one thought they could ever own, feeding from the palm of my hand at one moment, and then receiving me at his metal-toed feet as I knelt before him and his music filled the house like an army of violent angels residing in the speakers and golden flowers grew on vines twining around the chandeliers and spilling from the bedposts and banisters and jungle birds whistled in the fronds of potted palms and my art was myself—Violet Cassidy, girl-Jesus-vampire-angel-satan, concubine, mistress, wife of the *man.*

As you can see, I had lost it. I was pathetic. I was infatuated. And most definitely I was misled.

Sitting on the floor of my room with my hair pulled back in a ponytail, no makeup on my face, dressed in boys' boxers and a T-shirt, I felt completely different than the regular Violet. Claire and I were painting each other's toenails pale blue—not my normal choice, I only liked the dark metal Urban Decay colors—but I was in a blue toenail sort of frame of mind. (Claire was always.)

"Then what?" she asked again. I had told her about six times, a fact which I reminded her of, but she insisted.

"Then he gave me his address and he kissed my cheek and told me he thought I was brilliant and beautiful."

That was how our meeting ended. Flint Cassidy telling me I was brilliant and beautiful. Growling it, as if he were in pain. Looking at me like some kind of mortally wounded jungle animal who had come to rest his head in my lap and be mystically revived.

"I can't believe you have his address!" Claire cried. "You have Flint Cassidy's address!"

Claire was a blue toenails kind of girl, a squealing, feet-kicking kind of girl. I was not. At least not until that moment. I squealed, I kicked, we both did, ruining our baby-blue pedicures.

"Careful!" we squealed in unison. Was I becoming Tinker Bell after the brief but potent touch of Flint? That was when I confided in her, revealing the fantasy of the New Orleans mansion, the marriage bed, even some embarrassing thing about a wedding and a see-through lace wedding gown. (If you can't be an exhibitionist on your wedding day, then when?) But I was serious, and scared, and when she asked me what I was going to do I got very quiet and told her

I had no idea, which was another unusual thing for goal-oriented me.

"You have to go see him!" Claire said.

That night when she had fallen asleep on my bed, curled like a kitten and gripping the pillowcase, I sat up looking at myself in the mirror. I held the Spent Pleasure CD with Flint's face on the cover next to my reflection and imitated his petulant, girlish pout. His eyes were steely, his cheekbones dangerous. We could have been brother and sister. You you me me.

I whispered into the microphone of my tape recorder: "I told you you reminded me of me."

I hardly slept that night. I flopped around on the carpet like a fish while Claire dreamed of her enlightened race of faeries (I could tell by her expression of wonder) on my bed. In the morning I spent a long time getting ready—applying my makeup and choosing the perfect ensemble of halter crop top–hot pants–high go-go boots. Instead of black I opted for cherry-red satin. Some things I'd bought in a fit once months ago and never worn.

Now what, you may ask, was this girl thinking? And I am not only referring to my completely out-of-character fashion choice, not to mention how it clashed with my blue toenails (though they were hidden). That Flint Cassidy, some big thinks-he's-hot-shit rock star has slept with her and so suddenly she's acting like one of those crazed chicks she generally has so much contempt for? But you weren't there when we made love, this girl might respond. You weren't there when he looked into my eyes as if he had found the child-bride fallen girl-angel sweet vixen of his dreams. You weren't there when he whispered hoarsely, "My God, Violet, where did you come from? You are the most beautiful brilliant girl I've ever met." You probably aren't a girl who keeps trying to make life like a movie, either.

Still, what was I thinking? How naive was I? I didn't even become suspicious until I began to notice that all the buildings along that section of the street were businesses and not residential.

Maybe Flint Cassidy lived in a dazzling blue glass

office building? Maybe he called his penthouse "Metatalent" in honor of his own abilities? Maybe not, Vile.

He'd given me his agency's address, in case you haven't guessed by now. I hung a pissed off U-ie and headed back muttering about what an idiot I could be. But then a thought occurred to me.

Ambition.

Fatal flaw or life-saving energy channel? It had saved me from suicidal thoughts before, when I really was Vile. Without my dreams of grandeur—delusions, maybe, but it didn't matter—without them I might have perished long ago. Without my movie fantasies, I might have been another statistic of teenage suicide at thirteen, cutting up my arms with hearts and crosses until the blood filled the bathtub and my corpse was left behind like a felled graffiti-stricken tree. So if ambition had saved me before, I figured I would turn to it again. I had been remiss in losing sight of it for those moments with Flint. It was the only thing that was real for me. He certainly wasn't real. But

Metatalent, that was a different thing altogether. It towered above me, flashing in the morning sun. It was calling to me, "Violet, bring me your treatments, your screenplays, bring me your concepts, your visions."

It was the voice of ambition, the only voice I could rely on, and I was ready to answer it. I had a script to finish a.s.a.p.

After I had dropped off my screenplay with the bitchy woman who insisted they did not take un-solicited manuscripts until her boss, a deeply tanned silver fox, happened to pass by on his way to lunch and corrected her, promising me to peruse the material himself, I decided I might as well go to school. What a mistake. Miss Henderson wasn't thrilled about me sauntering in late, even though I did apologize.

"I'm surprised you bothered coming at all," she waaa-ed.

Even my second apology wasn't good enough. It might have been if I were dressed differently, but as

I've mentioned, Miss Henderson was not a fan of my wardrobe or the reactions it caused. Especially with this new red factor. She told me she didn't like my attitude and that I should go see Mr. Hurley, the principal.

"I had some business," I tried to explain.

"Well, you certainly do look like a *working* girl in that outfit," she wittily quipped.

I left them all to their joke. This situation of school was getting intolerable. I had to do something.

Claire tried to cheer me up. That night we went to Neo-Bo, as in Bo-hemian. We sat upstairs in the dark, slumped on one of the torn velvet couches, under a gaudy piece of art in a heavy gold frame that could have killed us if there had been an earthquake. I was smoking greedily and Claire was reading the *New Times,* glancing up occasionally at the goateed boys in black that passed by.

"How about him?" she said, jabbing an elbow into my rib cage.

"What?" I gloomily grumbled.

"For your love interest."

67

I glared at her. Sometimes her cheerfulness made me want to shriek. Or puke. Or shriek and then puke.

"It's not so bad," Claire said. "Maybe he thought you wanted his agent's address so you could give them your script."

I squashed my cigarette in the ashtray like I was killing a bug. "I did. That's what I wanted and I did, Claire," I enunciated.

She knew right away she was pissing me off. "Oh right. That's what I meant," she mumbled, going back to her newspaper.

I watched over her shoulder as she circled an ad that read, "Poetry for Screenwriters." There was a photo of a tall sad-eyed man with very large hands. Well, Claire could drool about poetry and laze away in cafes until she was old and gray. I, on the other hand, had places to go, people to meet. If Flint wasn't my guy it mattered not; my screenplay was in the world. I was sure it would bring me what I desired.

A week later I received a call from Metatalent; an agent named Richter wanted to meet with me. I assumed that he was Silver Fox. Since he had seemed more interested in my body than in my work, I wore my shortest black skirt suit for the occasion. I tried not to think about the possibility of running into Flint at the office. But he was probably in London or somewhere anyway, I told myself.

Flint was not my destiny. But Richter, that was a different story. When I walked into his office I felt something serious was going to happen. He had a tanning booth and a Universal machine in the room. His feet in their expensive thin-soled Italian leather shoes were up on the desk, his hands behind his sterling-haired head. He nodded for me to sit down when I held out my hand to shake. It seemed that Mr. Richter didn't shake easily.

"Well, Violet," he began, looking at something on the wall behind my head, "I do see some real talent here."

"Thank you, Mr. Richter."

"You need to learn a few things though," he went on, as if I hadn't spoken. "Do you know what high concept means?"

I did.

He looked at me then, with a molten heat in his dark eyes that made me flinch. "I used to think it meant lofty. Almost religious, do you know what I'm saying?" he asked fervently. Then his mood changed, briefly, to a wan melancholy.

"That was when I was young and innocent like you."

That part about the "innocent" pissed me off. Not to mention how he had ignored my handshake, avoided looking at me except when it most suited his delivery, and stepped all over my lines. And high concept bugged me.

"It's actually kind of a cheap thing," I retorted.

Richter's tepid melancholy changed to burning ice. "It's what we're looking for, Violet. It's what you need to work on."

I stuck out my chin, which looked defiant and

70

slightly jutting even in repose, and said, "I can learn."

This seemed to charm him. He leaned forward and gazed into my face. "We're not just interested in established talent. We're interested in nurturing budding young talent. How old are you, Violet?"

"Seventeen. But I'm . . ."

He was not put off by my age at all. In fact it made him beam. "That's excellent. That's what we're looking for. Youth sells these days. That *Kids* kid is *old* already."

I gave him my sweetest smile. I had been saving it for the right moment.

He said, "I think I can work with you."

I started to thank him but he put up a hand. "We're not going to represent you yet. You obviously have talent and ambition but you need more experience."

He leaned closer still, threatening. There was something manic in his face, the face of a man who would do anything to get what he wanted. Ruthless. I didn't want to let him see me pull back. I could learn something from this Richter.

71

"We need a new receptionist, Violet. I'd be willing to offer you that position if you're interested."

"I'm still in school."

"You can come in afterward."

I decided to play it as cool as possible. "And you'll look at my work?"

"Better than that. I'll give you input." He lowered his voice to a gentle gravelly growl. "You just have to trust me."

And then Richter did the thing that he had managed, by withholding it, to bestow with major significance; Mr. Metatalent himself reached out to shake my hand.

I saw the faintest gleam in his eyes when I hesitated before shaking his. I believe he had recognized that Violet Samms was a quick study.

Things were looking up. Every day after school dressed in my sexy but for-success outfits, I drove the 'Stang to the office where I served Richter and the other agents as if I had no interest in a career as a screenwriter but lived to answer the phones with the phrase, "Metatalent, can you hold." Occasionally I would attend a class at school, when the other part-time receptionist was around, but mostly I lived for my job. I made up for the lost hours that were being wasted at high school by working late, and on weekends, doing secretarial tasks for Richter. He said I was talented enough that he'd put up with my school schedule in order to have me as the "figurehead of the ship," as he called it. You might think that he'd want me to go to his office and dress the part of figurehead if you know what I mean, but he was quite respectful; I didn't have to disrobe and he never laid a finger on me. My salary was good and I was able to save most of it. At first I thought I'd like to use it for film school, but then I began to consider the possibility of funding my own production.

"After all, Robert Rodriguez made *El Mariachi* for like nothing!" I told Claire.

Another advantage of working at Metatalent was having contact with the awesome clientele. One day a certain very tall, very gorgeous, very famous couple who were supposedly divorced, came in holding hands. They were even taller in real life than they appeared on screen and in print. I found myself struck almost speechless when I had to announce their arrival. They were very nice about it, however. Thoughts about her mole kept me occupied for the rest of the day.

I told these things to Claire and she squealed. I felt so happy between my job, my friendship with Claire and the possibility of my film getting made that school was tolerable. I certainly didn't think about a certain pretentious self-coveting rock star. I knew he was ancient history when Claire passed me a note in Mrs. Hellberger's history class: "Are you going to look up his home address?"

I knew who she meant but I said "Whose?"

"You know . . ." she said.

"There was only one reason for me to have had that thing with Flint," I told her. "And that was to bring me to Metatalent."

Claire was worried about me, though. She thought I was working too hard. One day while we

74

were panting around the smoggy track at school, the jockettes whizzing by us at top speed and Coach Pitt angrily blowing her whistle, Claire asked if I was working on the movie.

"I've been a little distracted," I said. "But I'm sure it's all rubbing off on me in really excellent ways."

"Aren't you tired? You're working so much, Violet."

"I love it," I told her.

"I think you should do something to relax, though. To feed your spirit."

I informed her that was exactly what I was doing.

And then she sprang it on me. "No, I mean, like poetry. There's this poetry-writing workshop I want to take. Extension. It looks really cool. It's cheap, too."

She pulled an ad out from the pocket of her gym shorts. It said, "Poetry for Screenwriters." There was the photo of the tall, sad-eyed man.

I had to admit the screenwriters part interested me a little. But I was skeptical. "That's one way to sell a poetry workshop in L.A. It sounds a little bogus to me."

"He looks very sensitive. He looks like the kind of person you could share anything with."

I rolled my eyes. But I had to admit one thing. This guy could be a love interest for Claire's character in the movie.

"I wonder if he acts," I said.

If Peter Brookman acted it seemed like all he knew was one part; the soft-spoken, seemingly innocent seducer of young poets with faerie wings. We came into the classroom late and he smiled up at us, but his eyes lingered on Claire longer and last.

"Welcome, ladies," he said, after we'd told him our names. "Make yourselves comfortable."

I crossed every limb and glared at him from my seat. Claire leaned forward. She seemed to be holding her breath.

"First of all," Brookman said. "I'd like to know why you're all here. What does poetry mean to you."

A prematurely balding guy with thick-framed

glasses said, "I'm a screenwriter. I wanted to sharpen my sense of rhythm and imagery."

"Excellent," said Brookman, gesturing with his large hands. "I believe poetry can really do that for you. Is there anyone in here who isn't a screenwriter?"

After a long awkward pause Claire raised her hand.

"Claire, right?"

She nodded shyly.

"Why are you here, Claire?"

"I've written poetry since I was little. I thought it was like my secret language. And then I discovered that other people had been doing it forever and I was so excited. All I wanted to do forever was to read and write poetry and . . ."

She stopped, self-conscious. But Brookman reassured her.

"That's very beautiful. I've actually felt the same way myself."

I thought I might chuck up. How many times had he used that one? I rolled my eyes.

At that moment a tiny Chihuahua peeked its head out of Brookman's desk drawer. I figured he'd trained it to do that to punctuate his come-on lines. It looked like a muskrat more than a dog.

"I guess Lord Byron agrees," he said as everyone (especially our Miss Claire) giggled.

Lord Byron jumped out of the desk and ran in mad circles around the room. All I could think about was how once I'd read that Chihuahuas' eyes occasionally popped out of their heads and had to be re-inserted. Morbid, I know. But something about Brookman brought that out in me. I was worried about Claire, all of a sudden.

Jealousy? Was I jealous? I didn't know it then. Maybe if I had known it, things would have been different. All I knew was that I was feeling suddenly unsettled, as if something I needed in order to survive was about to be taken away.

It was not a feeling I could handle. I decided that I would hold on to the one thing no one could take from me—my work.

❖　❖　❖

The next day, Richter called me into his office where he was pumping iron and talking on a cell phone. He didn't get up but he wiped the sweat from his face and pointed over to his desk.

"The envelope, please."

I went over to pick up a small packet marked with my name. Richter got off the phone, still chuckling at his joke.

"One of these days I wouldn't be surprised if you're sitting there in that audience full of beautiful people, wearing the most devastating Alaia gown and you hear those very words followed by, 'And the best screenplay goes to . . . Violet Samms.'"

"Why?" I asked.

"Why?"

"Why do you think I'll win an Oscar?"

Richter got up from his bench press, threw a towel around his neck and stood watching me. His tone was patient if slightly condescending. "I've been in this business long enough to recognize raw talent when I see it, Miss. I hope you have more faith in me than that."

"Thank you, Mr. Richter," I said. I always tried to use his name. It seemed like a power-business type thing to do.

"Aren't you going to open your envelope, Violet?" (It seemed he was into power business too).

I already guessed what was there by the weight and the sound. I was right: keys. He must have seen my anxiety although I tried to hide it. I really hoped Richter wasn't trying to get me to sleep with him in order to keep my job.

But he reassured me. "No worries. They are keys to the office. Any time you need to come after hours and work on your writing, feel free. I want to stimulate your budding creativity."

The words "stimulate" and "budding" still worried me, but I got the feeling Richter's seduction wasn't as literal as, well, shall we say, literary. It seemed like if he really wanted to sleep with me he wouldn't have bothered with such an elaborate plan. And it might be a kick to work at the office some time alone at night; it might inspire an interesting story.

I figured that by focusing on my work I'd be able to ignore Claire's obsession with Brookman. I figured it would wane after a couple of days when she realized what kind of a guy he really was. But I was wrong.

We were sitting at the Raunch Room one night watching the boys mosh around in the pit and Claire wasn't drinking her soda or listening to the thrashing music but scribbling in a notebook. I asked her what she was doing and she said she was writing her assignment for Brookman. I told her we had a week.

"I feel so inspired! I can't stop thinking about that poem he read us. Isn't he beautiful?" she drooled.

"Who?" I said, lighting a cigarette. I mean, she *could* have been talking about someone else, a mosh-boy for example.

When she squealed Brookman's name I wished I hadn't asked the obvious. "He's all right if you like that type," I said.

81

I glanced over at the stage where just a short time ago Flint Cassidy had reeled and screamed like a boy-Violet in holey jeans. That type—that Brookman type—what a bore. I needed more excitement, I told myself.

Yes, more excitement. Maybe my need for excitement, for something to really happen in my dull life, combined with the jealousy that I couldn't acknowledge yet, was what made me vulnerable to the whim of my brutal muse—a sleek tan middle-aged fox in an Armani suit who had suggested, perhaps in response to my glum mood, that I use the office that night, see if a change of atmosphere might help my work. And I was up for a bit of a change, maybe a bit of adventure.

They say be careful what you wish for.

At first when I saw them in Richter's office, I thought, this can't be real. But what is it then? Am I taking after Judy? Am I insane? Or, *is* it real? Should I get the fuck out of here right now? But I didn't; I stayed. Violet Samms—always eager for a good story. He had counted on that. And I listened. And took note. The way he wanted.

Richter turned slowly toward the door and the petite blonde actress recovered merrily from her swoon. They looked at me. They laughed.

"What the . . ." I started to say. I have seen and heard of some pretty sick things in my young life, but this was one of the most original.

"Don't be upset, Violet," he said. "It's for you. A gift for you."

Richter's gift was a staging of an idea for a script: young Girl Friday, with wild ambition to write for the silver screen, stumbles across something in her agent-boss's office one night. As he's testing a hot babe for a scene in which she's murdered, things take a turn. It's no longer play acting, the murder is real. And all of the above is witnessed by Girl Friday, as was Boss-Guy's intent—she can't let anyone know— what will he do to her? But he's a sicky in more ways than one—he wants to make sure she gets it all on paper, she has a story to write for him now. High concept. Blockbuster. And, most especially, very, very wicked.

This was the story that opened the door to a different world. I'd always imagined that when that door opened it would lead to emerald citadels and lost utopian horizons, ghost towns swaggering with gun-toting cowboy idols and petticoat whores, swank palmy night clubs where six-foot-tall champagne bottles danced with bare-shouldered beauties, vistas made of paint, gauze and diamonds. But my story would not become a healing vision, a sublime dream, imprinted on the consciousness of an audience who longed to heal their damaged hearts in the darkness of a theater decorated like a palace or a shrine. My story would drip blood and make them writhe in their eight-dollar seats. I saw it everywhere I looked, imposed on the night like a drive-in screen glimpsed on a highway—a window through to another, bigger, even more violent universe.

What had Richter done? By using what I'd seen, did that make me guilty of something, too? And what would it do to me? Playing in the dark. Would I become Vile again, secretly collecting razor blades in an asylum and hiding them under my tongue to carve screenplays on my body?

All I knew was that I had to write till it was over. And so I wrote.

Fade to black.

Claire

I haven't written in my journal for an eternity. I just haven't been depressed enough, or happy enough. I know that's not the way a mature writer behaves, but I can't help it. I either have to be deliriously upset or deliriously in love. Well, now I'm kind of both.

The upset has to do with Violet. At first we raced through space, like shadows and light; her rants, my raves; her dark hair, my blond; black dresses, white. She a purple-black African-violet-dark butterfly and I a white moth. We were two wild ponies, Dawn and Midnight, the wind electrifying our manes and our hooves quaking the city; we were photo negatives of each other, together making the perfect image of a girl. Projecting our movie onto the sky.

Violet is strong like muscle and sinew and sophisticated like silk velvet, liqueur. I do think she has lived a number of other lives in which she learned how to look at things differently. She sees angles and light, she hears tones in voices, she watches stories unfolding when I'm not even aware that a story is taking place. (For Violet a story is always taking place.)

Violet believed that I had something too, some quality that no one had ever noticed in me before. And she defended me that day, with the sandwich. She didn't even question it. I mean, the reason they were harassing me wasn't just about the wings. It was the thing I said about faeries in class, how I said I think I'm a descendent of an ancient race who knew the secrets of nature and radiated light and were then forced underground and corrupted in the folklore into weak little flitty fantasy things. So I guess those kids had the right to bomb me for revealing something like that, but Violet didn't think so.

We were going to make our own movie. We were going to show the world itself the way we wanted it to be, and maybe then the world would turn into that place—a place where two girls rode a wild black Mustang through a night smeared with starlight, thick with butterflies.

But then this weird thing happened, and I'm still not even sure what it was. Something about that new part of the script Violet started writing ever since she got the job at that big agency. And now she's sold it for a fortune, but the change in her came before she sold it. It didn't seem to just be about the money. She was sort of troubled by something. And it's worse now. I can see it in her eyes like a little reel of film, playing over and over again. But I can't get close enough to see the images on the screen. I don't know what to do.

On top of that there is Peter Brookman. When I saw his picture in the ad, it was like finding the first piece of the jigsaw puzzle that would fill up the empty place in me, the place that had been growing and growing, bigger and emptier, since I was three, since my dad left. I don't remember my dad. But there is a sensation I have of someone tall standing in the shadows, of the smell of cigarettes and the texture of corduroy and a desire to be enveloped by the shadows and smoke and fabric, a desire to go with him when he left. I can't see his face. And my mom destroyed all the pictures—decapitating him in them. I just know that he left and she got fatter and

I got thinner, both of us with longing. That my heart closed. That I started feeling different, not human, part of the faeries, because real living girls were never this ice-cold and alone.

But every time I'm around Peter Brookman it's like another piece filling the emptiness. The finished puzzle is a tall poet with big hands and full lips and sad eyes that turn down at the corners, this man who carries a dog named Lord Byron around in his pocket and who asks me questions and reads the poetry that I write. Someday maybe the puzzle will be complete inside of me.

But between these two emotions—this weirdness with Violet and this need for my poetry teacher—I'm spinning. I can't seem to concentrate. It also has to do with making such a big move, I guess. L.A. is so different from the Midwest. Most people would just love the change—not being cold in the winter, so cold that your bones feel like rods of ice, ready to crack—and I do love the jacaranda trees, with their purple nipple-shaped blossoms and castanet-shaped pods, and the pink tassels hanging from the silk trees. It's also much nicer to be in a real house instead of the trailer park. I don't want to be ungrateful. If Aunt Meg hadn't died and left us this place, we'd still be living in that trailer with the fake flowers in the window box and the flimsy little wall separating my bed from Mom's. But I miss the fields full of puffy white Queen Anne's lace and the high stalks of corn where I could hide, making wigs for my dolls out of shiny yellow corn silk and plucking off the raw kernels to feed the birds. I miss how those same fields lit up with green electric sparks at night—fireflies, which to me are almost as magical as seeing faeries. Trying to catch them to wear in my hair. Here you don't see dream-eyed deer or rascal raccoons or the red baby foxes I found, boxing like puppies under the hill by the lake; here you see maybe just an occasional pigeon or squirrel. Everyone here is so beautiful and well-dressed and tan like TV ads and their cars are so new and lunar looking. They have mansions perched on stilts on the top of hills, in spite of the earthquakes, and huge gas-slurping cars even though they have to drive an hour to get anywhere, and they wear sunglasses all year long. Many of the flowers here are beautiful but also poisonous—oleander and belladonna. The air is poisonous, too, but deceptive, because at sunset it is rose and it shines, and at night it smells of jasmine. I want to go and hide in my abandoned barn that everyone said was haunted but where I felt safer than at school, writing poems by candlelight and hoping for ghosts, but it was always just cows or owls; or in the graveyard among the ancient headstones, making up stories about the dead. Like that little girl, Emily Mercy (1910–1919). I imagined her running with me through the cornfields, her long braids flying, her hands colder than marble. The kids at school thought I was weird, living in the trailer park with a mother who never spoke to anyone, spending all my time alone roaming the hills searching for signs of faerie homes. It's not that I literally think I'm a faerie. It's just that I feel so different from most people. And this idea of a race living underground in caverns, spending all their days dancing and playing the fiddle and eating flowers and reciting poetry and sharing their dreams, that to me sounds much more real than the way people live in this world, hating and fighting and wanting and hurting.

I still think a lot about those boys with the shotguns. I still dream about it. Running through the leaves crackling and crunching under my feet, my fingers ready to drop off with cold. Falling on the ground with my face smashed into the dirt, praying that they won't see me, that the earth will crack open and let me in.

Here no one chases me with shotguns, but I'm afraid of them anyway. Except for Violet.

That's why I was so glad when she agreed to go to Joshua Tree with me. I've always wanted to see the desert. And it will be good for her, I think, and give me the chance to write and catch up on all the things I'm feeling.

There is no way to describe the desert in regular language. I want to make up a new language for it. Peter Brookman says that is what poetry is to him— "a self-made language of the heart with which to describe the indescribable."

Did you know that the Joshua trees are not really trees at all but a kind of lily? Like the flower in the annunciation. The graceful creamy bell that the angel gave to Mary to announce the mystical conception, as if the secret of the birth was trumpeting up from inside the petals. I read that Joshua trees are a descendent of that flower.

We drove out there in Violet's car. It feels good to get away from the city. It felt as if we'd really escaped when we got to the life-sized dinosaurs at Cabazon. One's expression reminded me of something Peter Brookman's Lord Byron does with his teeth sometimes. In a way it was sad to think that the only dinosaurs left are tourist attractions marking the place where you can buy candy bars, but still I was glad they were there, casting their huge shadows onto the violet-colored mountains. Then we saw the windmills spinning manically all over the hills like fallen stars trying to get back home. The air tasted hot-dry-clean and my ears started to pop as we climbed into the higher altitudes.

Violet turned off the highway and we bumped along over this dirt road, past more Joshua trees. The sun was setting and the sky was this glorious shade of pink, and forever. We found an empty campground and lay our sleeping bags out under the Joshua trees. I started to build a fire and Violet asked how I knew how to do that. I was glad she seemed a little interested in something, so I told her about playing in the woods and how sometimes it got so cold that the only way I could avoid going back to the trailer was to learn to build a campfire. We sat near ours, as close as we could get without burning up. In the firelight Violet looked beautiful, spooky and flickering; she still didn't say much. We roasted marshmallows for dinner and licked the charred sugar goo off our fingers. Then we weren't sure what else to do and the fire was dying, so we got into our sleeping bags.

It was hard for me to sleep because the moon was so bright, but I could hear Violet's breathing and I knew she was sleeping, which was good; I don't know how much sleep she has been getting lately. I felt lonely, though, with her asleep, really empty. I wondered what Peter Brookman was doing and if he'd read my latest assignment, and if he were here if the space in me would feel filled up. I wish I wasn't a girl who needed so much but a little free creature that slept in deserts and ran on clouds and lived on lilies.

In the morning when I opened my eyes a desert bunny was watching me. I elbowed Violet to show her, but when she turned over, it ran away. Part of me wanted to follow it like Alice in Wonderland and see where it took me, but I was pretty hungry; so instead of looking for rabbit holes I made coffee and got out the bananas and bagels we'd brought.

Violet got up and went to sit on a rock in the sun.

I brought her food, but she only wanted coffee. I told her I was worried; it seemed like she hadn't been eating at all.

She just shrugged and picked up her *Variety*— the one with the article about her in it, of course: "TEEN SCREENWRITER CUTS 6-FIGURE DEAL." It was obvious she didn't want to talk, so I chased this yellow butterfly that was flitting around.

After a while I noticed Violet was watching me.

I said, "I love it out here. Maybe we should move."

"There's not much of a film community," she said.

I told her we could make our own movies. About faeries.

This made her roll her eyes and I got mad. I went into my same old speech about how the faeries were serious, how a few of them had survived the holocaust and that some of us were descended from them. I told her that I thought Peter Brookman was.

"I hope he's not a faerie, for your sake!" Violet said.

99

I thought it was a pretty stupid joke, but I could tell she was upset that I'd brought him up so I ignored it.

That therapist they sent me to once said I need to forget about the faeries and realize that I am a real live girl, that I can't live on ice and scraps; but I'm afraid if I become real, I'll be like my mother—bloated and sad. I'd rather chew morsels and suck flowers and wear feathers. I never want to be like her. She used to be this fragile girl who believed my father had given her wings. I'd seen pictures of her from then and read the love poems she'd written to him. He was her professor at the university. He came into that small town with the cobblestone streets, like one of the beautiful men on the posters on her walls come to life, told her her essays were good, told her about what it was like outside of Ohio, beyond the cornfields, gave her books to read. She was a little freshman, a little country girl living in a trailer park, but she had heard the Beatles, she had read Kerouac. And she had met him—my father. A huge dark-shouldered silhouette against a sky swollen with summer rain. That's what I imagined. A voice reading her words that made her heart explode like the sky when rain finally came. And she was lying in a field of Queen Anne's lace and fireflies, she was staring at the constellations and listening to him quoting Walt Whitman. His love could fly her away anywhere, she believed. But then after only a few years he flew alone. She had to move out of the house and back to the trailer park. She was left thinking about California because it was warm and because he had spoken about the way you'd never be cold like in the Midwest. Your blood turns to honey, he said. Your blood turns to the blue Pacific. The rock stars and film stars live in the canyons in houses with gardens full of plants that have aphrodisiac properties. Big sparkling glass windows reverberate with drumbeats, while the city lights keep the beat below. Spotlights fan back and forth across the sky all night long. He was going to California, maybe, she thought. She'd go there, too, with me when she had enough money.

Leave the trailer park. Then Meg died and left us the house. But by that time my mom had changed so completely he would never have recognized her, even if she'd been able to find him. She didn't recognize herself.

I am so afraid of the changes pain can cause.

Later on, Violet and I went hiking and we found this creek filled with the water that comes down from the mountain. It's amazing to see snow-capped peaks when it's so warm below. I begged Violet until she finally took off her jeans and got in with me. The water rushed over us, cold and glinty, foamy and churning. Our lips were almost as blue as the sky, but it felt good with the warm sun on our shoulders. We lay on the rocks to dry and I wished that I could tell Violet about my feelings for Peter so that she would understand.

It is a need on a cellular level, something I couldn't give up for anything. Something I'd been born with, maybe, the way you need food or sleep or your parents when you are a baby. Or maybe something that came to me later, when my dad left and my mom's heart followed him.

But I couldn't tell Violet about Peter, so instead I said, "I wish we never had to go back. I wish we could stay out here forever." I didn't add, "Maybe Peter would come, too," but I thought it.

Of course we had to go back. I had to go back to my sad mother and her dusty house stuffed with decapitated photographs, and school where they thought I was a freak. Luckily Violet and Peter would be there, too. If they weren't in my life I couldn't have handled going back at all.

What do I really mean by that? What would I do if I really couldn't handle something? Violet told me how she used to cut herself with razor blades, never deep enough to die, but just to see what she was like inside. I've never been brave enough to hurt myself, although I've thought about it before.

I think if I ever really wanted to hurt myself I would put myself in a situation where someone else would do it to me. Like the time the boys chased me through the woods, pretending I was a deer.

I hate school so much. Violet was out again today so I ate lunch alone. That guy Steve came up to me with his friends and said, "Hey, where's your famous girlfriend? Is she too famous to come to school now?"

One of the boys said, "You'll make her cry, Steve. Maybe her friend dumped her for some hot Hollywood babe."

I got up and walked away and then I felt something hard crack against my temple and then it shattered wet and slimy. It was an egg. I kept thinking, this little dead baby chicken embryo is dripping in my hair and down my arms.

I went into the girls' room and threw up. I kept thinking of the time in the sixth grade when Bitty Risher and Alison Kettler concocted a slop out of all the cafeteria leftovers and made me eat some. I could still see it and smell it when I got sick.

When I was quiet I heard some girls imitating my retching noises and laughing outside the stall. I knew that if Violet were there everyone would have left me alone.

Sometimes compared to school my mom seems okay. She asked me if I've been writing. Once in a while she gets lucid like that and seems to understand. I said a little. I didn't want to tell her about Brookman's class, because of the money. Even though I'm taking it for free, helping him out on the computer and stuff. But I didn't want any questions from her. Anyway, she did say, "Oh my, Claire. You must always keep writing. It's all you have, isn't it?" Her hair was stringy and in her eyes, and her skin was blotchy and pale and her arms were mottled, droopy with flesh.

"It's all you have, isn't it?"

Maybe she's right. Somehow, I'm not comforted.

This afternoon I heard a knock on the door, and when I opened it I saw Violet's car driving away. And on the porch were all these presents! I couldn't believe it. There were beautiful gauzy faerie dresses and a whole flock of Sky Dancers, those plastic dolls with wings that really fly. I guess Violet had gotten her check and it was so cool of her to do that, but I didn't know why she drove away.

When I called to thank her she said she was going to this big party. I asked her if I could go. She seemed hesitant, but then she said okay.

The whole thing was a mistake. There were all these fancy cars and valets and the house was a big white villa with vines growing all over the walls and a huge green lawn and palm trees lit up very surreal. Inside the rooms were painted chartreuse, coral or ultraviolet, and all these very tall very tan people were milling around and drinking. The glass of ice water I'd been clutching had penetrated my whole body, and I started to shiver. Violet got swept away by some "Suits," as she calls them. They all had severe haircuts and smelled like stinky cologne made from some poor animal's sex glands. I wanted to grab her away from them; I didn't like the way they were acting with her—turned on and condescending at the same time. She seemed more strung out than ever.

"Are your parents in the biz?" asked Suit #1.

"I read she was completely self taught," mused Suit #2.

"Would you teach me, Violet?" gawked #3.

They started laughing, and it wasn't with her, let me tell you.

These two supermodels came over to sneer and tweeze at the buffet. I kept staring at them because you rarely see creatures like that except in magazines, and they were so sleekly gorgeous as to be almost alienish. I was feeling the way I do in this dream where there are stains from my period on my white dress. In fact I almost wanted to ask Violet if there was a stain on me. I just wanted to leave so badly. Then this tan man with silver hair came over to Violet and she got this weird look on her face. I'd never seen Violet look like that so I wasn't even sure what emotion it was.

But I knew what I was feeling. What I was feeling was fear. It was like some kind of little hand moving around in my throat. I went over there and told her I wanted to leave.

The man asked who I was, and I told him because Violet didn't seem to want to. I wondered if she was ashamed of me. I had intentionally worn the dress she gave me so she wouldn't be.

"Pleased to meet you, Miss Claire, I like your dress," said the man, so I guess the dress wasn't the problem, but Violet still didn't introduce me.

"Violet got it for me," I said. "She's the best friend in the world." I wanted to make her feel better.

Before the man could say anything else, she grabbed my hand and pulled me away from him. Her fingernails dug into me. The way she held me she didn't seem ashamed, more sort of protective.

I asked her what was up but she wouldn't answer.

I was so glad to finally be out of there. It felt like I hadn't taken a breath for about an hour because of the little hand blocking my throat.

changeling

they wanted her back. to put in their puddings.
sup from her throat.
catch in the web
of their fingers.
she tried to speak softly
so they wouldn't find her.
tried to stay
the size of her bones.
this made their thirst grow
like a castle of salt.
their hunger devouring
like a castle of teeth.
and she couldn't help it. her words spilled
onto the page at night
like organs peonies
dead ponies.
calling them.

they wanted her.

once mother was too thin too.
pale always cold.
shredding insect wings beneath the covers.
dissecting flowers 'til they screamed.
now she is large and warm
dripping blood each month.

is it better to grow
full and bleed?
stay here in the world
of grief lungs anger livers intestine fear?

come with us, they whisper.

mother knows
that poetry is dangerous
essential.
she hands her a pen
gets bigger each day
at night removes her heart
to guard the door.

I wrote this poem about growing up and me and my mom and faerie, about how poetry is the one thing that both draws the faeries to you and keeps you safe from them. And in a way they are death, because they are escape from the real world into a kind of oblivion. But there is another death, and that is the death of being alive and becoming a woman and getting old, and the faeries are a way to escape that, too. I probably would never have written the poem if it wasn't for Peter Brookman, and I think it is the best one I've written. So now I love him even more for being my muse and my guide. And he liked it so much that not only did he ask me to read it out loud in class, but he also told me that he wanted to talk about it with me after class and would I like to go on a picnic with him. I feel like I'm going to explode, flying out of the withered cocoon of my old self.

I haven't seen Violet for a week. She isn't at school or in Peter's class, and she doesn't answer my calls. I have this present I want to give her. It isn't much, not like all the cool stuff she gave me, but it is a Tinker Bell night-light that glows in the dark, and

I thought it might comfort her and help her sleep better. The last time I saw her she looked like she wasn't sleeping too well, from the purple shadows under her eyes. I should go over and see what is up, but to tell you the truth I've been so obsessed with Peter Brookman that I guess I've kind of neglected her. I'm going to go over there, though.

I prepared for our picnic the entire week. I painted my nails five different pastel shades—one for each finger—and gave myself a facial and deep-conditioned my hair and washed and ironed the Violet dress. So I was reading my poem and right in the middle of it, right when I could feel Peter Brookman looking at me in a different way, when he was looking at me like that, Violet walked into the room. And when I saw her I realized how worried I'd been and I felt so badly that I hadn't gone to see her. She was all pale and she looked like she'd lost weight. I got up and went over to her and told her how worried I was and how I'd been trying to reach her, and why hadn't she returned my calls?

Peter told me to finish my poem, but I asked if I could do it next week and walked out of the room with Violet. I didn't even care if it would piss Peter off, because I could tell Violet really needed to talk.

In the hallway she broke down and started crying as soon as I asked her what was wrong. I didn't know what to say, so I said something lame about how it was just stupid Hollywood and she was too good for it and not to let it affect her so much. Then I gave her the Tinker Bell that I'd been carrying around and she seemed to really like her. She clutched her the way a little girl would, and that was so not like Violet. It reminded me of me for a second. But then Peter came out and he was looking kind and worried, not mad at all, and I said, "Violet?" and she said, "It's nothing. I'll be all right. I just wanted to see you."

Then I remembered the date, which believe it or not, I'd forgotten about for a few minutes, and I felt really bad and I asked Violet if she would come with us on this picnic. But when I said that, it really freaked her out and she took off. I called after her, but I didn't go running. There was this pull I was feeling from Peter like he was the refrigerator and I was one of those stupid magnets—a little weak girl with wings that were completely useless in helping her fly away.

He took me to the fountain at the base of Griffith Park. We were surrounded by the soft green mist of trees and the water was lilting in the streetlamp light. I could smell the jasmine and Peter's hair. His shampoo was like mint and green apples. We were eating pasta salad with lime and cilantro and drinking sparkling lemonade. I was intoxicated by everything, with the crescent of moon hanging above us like a charm—and the spray on my face that felt like a spray of moonlight as much as water.

"Since I was a kid I've always felt like this alien or something," Peter said. "Like I was from another planet. It sounds really pretentious, but poetry was the only way I felt I could kind of begin to communicate."

I told him I felt exactly like that. I told him I feel

like such a freak most of the time.

And he actually said, "But you're so pretty and talented."

I felt really embarrassed and I said, "Maybe you just think that because we came from the same planet or something."

And he said, "On my planet you are a beauty queen."

I had to sort of change the subject, but not too much, so I asked him what it was like there, on his planet.

"You can remember if you try." He was looking deep into my eyes, like the planet was inside of me.

So I told him about how you can talk to the animals and they can talk back and no one eats meat and everyone plays a musical instrument and in the morning you all tell each other your dreams. And he added about how everyone speaks in poetry and wears clothing made of rainbow-colored light and there isn't any sickness or poverty or hate.

Then I really had to get away from him or I was

afraid I'd start declaring my love or something so I hiked up my dress and waded into the fountain. He called for me to come back and said I'd get cold but I wouldn't come, so then he did something I didn't think he'd do—he took off his heavy brown Oxfords and his socks and rolled up his trousers and he got this determined look on his face and he started to wade over to me. So I splashed him and he splashed back. Then he grabbed my arms and held me and I could feel his pulse and everything was twinkling from the drops of water and the lights. It was like *La Dolce Vita,* Peter's favorite movie. (I'd rented it the day he told us that in class). We were Anita and Marcello, although, actually, Violet was the only one who really looked like someone from that movie— Anouk Aimée. But in my mind I was the movie goddess of his dreams. He picked me up in his arms and carried me out of the fountain, and we didn't speak the whole way back to his apartment.

It was tiny and messy with books everywhere, coffee cups, a few posters, including Gustav Klimt's kissing lovers, which is my favorite painting. I used to have a card of it over my bed in the trailer. When I broke our silence and told him how I loved it, he said that I looked like her—the girl dreaming in the man's arms like some kind of broken fabulous lily. I turned around from the poster and looked at him. He has broad shoulders and a strong neck like the man in the painting. He handed me a towel and I wrapped it around my head and leaned toward him. He rubbed my hair gently. Then he stopped and let the towel drop around my shoulders and looked into my eyes and kissed me.

He kept kissing me. Until my lips softened into his the way it felt when I used to kiss flowers when I was little, but so much better—this density and then this give and this feeling of falling, and he lifted me in his arms and carried me to the futon.

Then he started to kiss my neck and down, his hands moving inside my dress and I felt like I was going to be sick. His eyes were different, predatory and blank like a hunter's.

I can't explain why I couldn't. But all I knew

then was I had to be away from him, lying in a field somewhere with lupine in my mouth, butterfly wings pressing against my eyelids.

Faerie—hoarse how they whisper, light how they trip down. Untouched untouched untouched. The only way I could stay with them, stay safe.

Because what if I let him inside me and I thought the emptiness was gone and then he left? What kind of terrible emptiness would tear open then?

The next night he called and said, "It's okay, sweetie."

I apologized, too, and I said I guessed he didn't want to see me again. He said, no, he still did, I was his faerie princess and he just wanted to bask in my presence. He really did use the word bask. I was so happy because I do still feel so much for him. I just can't let him touch me that way yet. He must care about me, too, to still want to see me.

It's been only once a week, but the rest of the time I keep busy preparing. I try to write poems that will move him. I blow soap bubbles and make gauzy dresses and shop for shoes at thrift stores and dance around my room and paint my toenails with glitter polish and read books he has recommended and rent videos he likes. That is why I haven't called Violet. I am tripping out in my own little Peter Brookman universe. She hasn't called me either.

I was sitting on campus today and someone came up and put their hands over my eyes and at first I jumped thinking of eggs and names and guns, but then I smelled Violet's dusky lovely perfume. I said her name, and she apologized for freaking me out like that. We just looked at each other for a little while. She seemed a lot older and was wearing these very expensive-looking silver leather jeans and these silver engineer boots with steel toes. I didn't know what to say to her except how I'd been worried and where'd she been? All of a sudden I felt really shitty that I hadn't called, even if she hasn't called me either. She told me she dropped out of school. Then she asked what I was doing tonight and I told her

I was seeing Peter and she should come with us.

But she told me she was having a housewarming party. I didn't know she had moved. It felt weird that she hadn't told me.

"We would have helped you," I said, but she said it was all done and that I should come by. She didn't mention Peter at all.

I asked her how she was, and she made this hard face and said, "I'm great. I decided I better start enjoying my new life."

Then she gave me her address and left.

All of a sudden this worry hit me. Harder than before. I wondered if she was doing drugs? Or if the pressure was just too much for her. I didn't get it.

I asked Peter if we could go to Violet's thing after the movies. It was in this icy-looking condo above the Sunset strip. Lots of dark glass and cold metal. Lots of hipsters, the new young Hollywoodites and -ettes in all their tattooed glory. Also that idiot Steve from school crashing a few of his friends. I couldn't believe he'd actually dare to show up after all the things he said. He gave me this big smirk when he saw me. But luckily I was with Peter so I didn't care.

Peter and I felt kind of weird. I thought we'd feel better when we saw Violet, but it was worse. She had on this very sexy red dress and her eyes were all glazed, like the surfaces of her apartment. She kept rubbing her skin, like she was trying to remove some invisible substance. On the stereo that song "Girl Satan" by creepy Flint Cassidy was blasting and Violet was dancing around to it. I went over to her and tried to hug her but she just handed me her drink and danced away. Someone pulled her into a room and I followed her. She was on the bed, tangled up with these very beautiful cocaine-colored kids, snorting powder off a mirror, staring at her reflection like she was trying to inhale herself. Then she closed her eyes and ran her tongue over her teeth and lips and smiled. When she opened her eyes they were too bright and almost electric-looking. I asked if I could talk to her for a second and she just started laughing. I told her I was serious and she wiped her nose and just looked at me and I took her hand and pulled her out onto the patio. The light was trippy and poison green. "Dancing Barefoot" by Patti Smith started playing and Violet lifted her arms over her head and spun around like a kid trying to make herself dizzy. Then she sort of started to collapse into the tropical flowering plants. I grabbed her like a tango partner, supporting her in my arms, and told her I was worried.

She said, "Worried. Why would you be worried? You have Brookman. Besides, worry builds character. It'll give you something to write about."

I said, "Why are you acting this way?"

And she said, "You could never understand, babe. You are living in your own little world."

I asked her what that scene *there* was.

"This is the real world," Violet said. "And I belong to it now."

And then, for the first time, she lost me. She was this weird cold power-machine, and I didn't care anymore. That happens to me sometimes when someone hurts me. I seem all mushy and a crybaby and weak, but when someone hurts me everything changes. My heart shuts like a fortress and nothing can open it. That started when I was old enough to realize that my dad had left. It's a physical sensation in my chest, a hardening, a heaviness. Wood planks and chains and metal locks. It frightens me. It frightens me as much as anything anyone has ever done to me.

I should have known that Peter would do what he did. I am used to men going away. Like my dad. So why should Peter be any different? Peter talked about poetry and he talked about our planet, so I thought he was different, but it was all just my lame fantasy.

The way it happened is so stupid and cliché. I'd had a really bad day at school. One of those days where whenever anyone asked me anything in class my head would pound like a heart, and I felt like there was a heart stuck in my throat. Then I was doing my laps around the track in p.e. and Kaylie Rogers and her friends ran past me, and one of them stuck out her foot and tripped me and I went flailing face-first into the dirt. It brought up memories of the hunt, and I had to lie there for a second, not 'cause I was physically hurt but to keep from letting them see me cry. They saw it anyway, of course. Once, Violet had said it was good that I cried easily; actresses should be able to do that. I knew she said it just to make me feel better; a real actress should have been able to hide the tears, to get up and flip off Kaylie and her friends and strut away like she was going to a movie premiere with her gorgeous boyfriend. Then I missed Violet, remembering that. The way we'd been before. They wouldn't have touched me if she were around.

But I remembered what it had been like at her party, so instead of going to see Violet I went home and cleaned myself up and made some food and went over to Peter's apartment. He came to the door barefoot, with his shirt untucked and his hair standing up on his head. Lord Byron was peeping out from between his legs, wagging. I handed Peter a red rose I'd poached on the way, and told him I had made us a picnic.

He said, "You should have called, Claire."

I told him I wanted to surprise him and he said he couldn't see me right then. He wouldn't look me in the eye, and then I felt the bomb ticking in my chest. I looked down—there were two pairs of shoes by the door—Peter's Oxfords and a pair of high-heeled sandals. Unfortunately for Peter I am a very observant shoe fetishist. I recognized the sandals from the feet of the new girl in class. The one who had read her poem the week before: "I was a Medieval/patient/swollen with/poison/You were the physician/applying leeches/burning glasses/to my flesh./Freeing me/from myself." Melanie. I had noticed how Peter stared at her when she read. I had noticed her big breasts and long red hair and leechy lips. I had noticed her sandals. I knew she was in there, languishing on his bed, waiting for him to suck the poison out of her.

He called my name as I dropped the basket and ran down the stairs. But he didn't run after me. And I waited for the bomb in my chest to explode.

It didn't. If it had, it might have blasted the wall

there and I would have been able to feel something, but instead I just got cold. Ice-cube cold, corpse cold.

I didn't think I'd go to see Violet, then. But I didn't know what else to do. I was afraid to go home. If I saw my mom's weepy eyes and sad skin I was afraid I'd just start turning into that right then. That I'd just get locked up in this house with her, both of us miserable and bitter and pining until we died. So I went toward the person who I knew would never let pain make her ugly or weak or ruined. For Violet, pain is something you can use to make you strong. And it is what I needed, what I need, to believe.

Also, I love Violet. It hit me for the first time, then. I love her for that strength. I love her for knowing so much about movies, and being able to write like that, and for her style and her brilliant belligerence. I love how we could giggle together like kids, painting each other's toenails, and how Flint Cassidy had made her turn into a teenybopper and how she is the faerie queen, reminding me of what we had once been and could become. Also, she is the first person that has really believed in me. I thought Peter did, but I guess not.

It had hurt me to see Violet at the party, that other way, with the cocaine. But I told myself it was just the drugs, and no wonder she needed them. A queen of faerie needed a lot of help to live in a world that had banished all that was true and powerful and truly beautiful. I hadn't helped her; I'd abandoned her for Peter. I thought maybe I could help her now.

When I saw her, though, I just started crying.

My favorite Tori Amos song, "Bells for Her," was playing: *"I've got your mind I said she said I've your voice I said you don't need my voice girl you have your own but you never thought it was enough . . ."* I sat down on Violet's cold black floor and I couldn't stop; the tears felt thick and hot and red like blood. Finally, I heard Violet's voice at the periphery and she was saying, "I'm sorry I'm sorry," over and over again. And her pain sounded worse than mine so I shut up and just listened to her.

She said, "Claire, you're my best friend. You're my

only friend. I just went crazy. I can't explain it."

For the first time I heard tears in Violet's throat. They scared me. How would it be to cry after almost a lifetime of never crying?

I wiped my eyes and nose with my dress and looked at her. She had sort of crumpled in on herself. I wondered if I was wrong about pain making her stronger. But I loved her anyway. Maybe we could make each other stronger.

"I don't know what I did wrong," I said.

"You didn't do anything wrong. I'm the fucked up one." She asked what had happened, was it Brookman?

"Bells and footfalls and soldiers and dolls brothers and lovers she and I were now she seems to be sand under his shoes there's nothing I can do," Tori sang.

I just started crying again so Violet knelt down beside me and put her arms around me. They were thin but strong, Violet's arms. Clad in sheer black netting. Her hair fell around us, dark and jasmine silk. I could feel the pulse in her throat.

She took something out of her pocket; it was a

little glass vial and she told me it was a flower remedy.

"Holly for vexations of the heart. Rock rose for states of panic. Sweet chestnut for despair. Star of Bethlehem for grief or trauma."

She sounded like Ophelia.

I said, "Eating flowers? You're getting as weird as me. I told you you were a faerie."

We both laughed, and then she said how she'd gone to this chiropractor who wore a white turban and had eyes with every color of the forest in them. He'd fed her the essence of flowers and was helping her get clean.

"I told him how I acted at the party," she said. "I've been sick about it. I'm really trying to change things, Claire."

I tipped back my head and opened my mouth and she squeezed a few drops of the flower essence under my tongue.

Then I went to lie on Violet's bed and write this in my journal. I'm not sure if the flower essences really work or if I am just feeling better from the cry and being held, but suddenly I'm all drowsy. I can feel the faeries beckoning me into the peaceful poppyfields of sleep where boys never betray you or shoot at you and best friends tuck you in the folds of their wings until there is no difference between the two of you, and there is no sorrow and there is no pain.

Violet
&
Claire

When Claire woke up Violet was typing at her computer, with a rigid look to her jaw and her hands like claws. Claire asked her the time and she said eight-thirty and Claire wanted to know if she felt like going out for coffee, but she said she couldn't, she had work and she had to go to this party later. And that Claire could go with her.

Claire had thought Violet was trying to get away from all that, but Violet said she just had to finish up this one project, and then they'd be off her back and she could do what she wanted, *they* could do what they wanted, she corrected herself. Claire told her parties like that made her feel weird and Violet said they made her feel weird, too, but that she had to go. Claire said maybe she'd meet her, that she had to go home first and take care of a few things. The thing she wanted to take care of, really, was seeing Peter Brookman. She wanted to get all dressed up and stop by his house and tell him what she thought of him. It would be a tough Violet thing to do, Claire figured.

Then she'd probably feel strong enough to go to the party.

So she went home and put on dark lipstick, the kind Violet wore; Claire had borrowed it from her. She'd also borrowed a tight black corsetlike dress in case she decided to go the party. She hardly recognized herself dressed up like that. It felt good, though. It felt different from her mom and different from herself. Claire didn't want to look like anyone who had ever been hurt that badly, or abandoned or betrayed. She wanted to look like the one who did the betraying.

But, later, Claire thought, I was wrong. The lipstick and the dress weren't enough to switch things around. And the love she had felt, that wasn't enough to break any spell.

After she'd gotten dressed she rode over to Peter's house on her bicycle. The dress poked her rib cage and made it hard to breathe. There was a weird witchy wind shaking through the eucalyptus leaves and the moon was full and mean-neon-white.

Claire took her time, circling through the neighborhoods, trying to peek in the lit windows to see people watching their TVs or washing their dishes. She wished she had a little yellow house of her own, with a flower box full of real flowers and herbs—pansies and rosemary—and a sweet lover who would swing dance with her in the evenings and cook pasta and read poetry aloud. She thought that maybe she should try to be more like Violet, and wish instead for money and power and fame, but Violet wasn't happy either. Maybe we should run away together, Violet and I, Claire thought, go to the desert and try to catch falling stars in our mouths.

Driving through the night on her way to Peter Brookman's, Claire's mouth didn't taste like stars; it tasted like metal, like when she had braces when she was thirteen. It was a taste like dread.

One of those Schwarzenegger mobiles, those Desert Storm Hummer things, was parked out in front of Peter's apartment. Claire thought how funny it would be if Melanie drove one of those horrible things. She'd tell Violet about it and they'd crack up, speeding off past the giant dinosaurs and the windmills, off to the desert in the black Mustang convertible.

Because Claire was thinking that, she felt confused when she got closer. She saw Peter first, and that made sense. Even though it did seem weird that Melanie could afford a Hummer. But it wasn't Melanie at all. The girl driving the car, the girl Peter was saying good-bye to, was Violet.

Claire saw her hair, glossy and dark in the streetlamp light, and she saw the side of her face and she saw Peter standing there, the silhouette of his shoulders against the trees, neither of them real to her, like two characters in a film, suddenly. Because she couldn't feel any emotion like loss or betrayal or pain because she was dead. She was a Hummer. She was steel-toed boots and bullets and knives. She was hard cold metal.

The faeries fear anything metal, Claire remembered. If you want to curse them, keep them away from you,

you have to do spells with metal. And now Claire was that very thing, the very thing that would kill her. The wings were disintegrating. The petals were furling up. The leaves were burning. Claire stepped from the fire transformed, heartless, her whole body a weapon against itself.

When Violet saw Claire's face peeking at them from the darkness like some kind of peaked tree spirit, she changed, too. The change had started when Claire came to her, earlier that evening, crying, and Violet had known that Richter and Hollywood didn't matter now. She would go to this last party and turn in the rewrite he and the producer wanted and get paid, and after that, she and Claire would go away. Suddenly all she cared about was her friend, and the desert where they could buy an adobe house with Joshua trees all around and barbecue corn over an open fire and swim in the moon and maybe make their own films. It was such a relief to see Claire's face. It was like she had been floating through outer space, landed on a desolate planet,

137

and found, among the craters and dunes of nothing-ness, her lost astro-sister.

The thought of Brookman hurting Claire in any way had made Violet taste something liver-green. She had to go tell him. Maybe it was a way to chastise herself, too, for pulling away from Claire the way she had. The things she planned to say to Brookman were words she needed to say to herself. And also, going to him might have been a way for Violet to get close to something Claire loved, for one last time, to understand what it was Claire had needed so much.

She wasn't really aware of any of this, though, when she stopped at Brookman's apartment on the way to the party. All she knew was that she hated him and she wanted to tell him that he had hurt her friend, and to never come near Claire again. It felt like being inside the script again, like none of it was quite real but that she couldn't stop herself from it.

What she hadn't expected was that her anger

would have turned into something else. Because they were both furious with themselves and because they both loved the same girl and because she frustrated them with her innocence, as if she were too pure for the world. They had argued for a while and he had admitted to being a shithead and when Violet had tried to leave, he had asked her to stay for some coffee. He was worried about her, too, he said. Ever since this whole Hollywood thing. Then, suddenly, Violet had wanted to confide in Peter Brookman. He seemed strong enough to take it, the whole story, the reveal, as they said in town. And he was crazy enough himself that he wouldn't have judged her, she felt. And he might even comfort her, this man whom Claire had loved, and who still (she really believed) loved Claire. She had to tell someone.

Instead, she had let him kiss her.

Before it happened they had been talking for a while and she had started to say what had happened but she couldn't do it. He had asked why she was so sad and she had mumbled something about this scene she was caught up in and he had said she should just walk away.

"Yeah, just say no, right? What do you know about it?"

Then he had rolled up his sleeve and showed her the track marks on his forearm—marks he had never shown Claire, thinking they would frighten her, that she wouldn't understand—and Violet had wanted to touch them and show him her own scars from where she had cut herself. She had thought about the cocaine and asked if it was hard for him to quit.

"Easier than nicotine, honestly. But you are a tough girl."

"I need a cigarette."

"You just had one. They're not good for you."

"Oh, excuse me, Mr. Cub Scout."

"I can't help it," Peter had said, smiling, almost wincing, the way someone in pain smiles, and she had told him how much he reminded her of Claire right then, and how fucked it was that he had blown it with her.

"You're right, Violet, about it being fucked of me. But I think I'm more like you than like Claire."

"We're totally different. You have no ambition whatsoever."

"But I have desires that mess me up and make me forget about other people's feelings."

Violet had stared at him then, at the planes of his long, bony face, his deep-set eyes, his full, almost clownish mouth. She had wanted to tell him but she couldn't tell him.

"I've got to go," she had said.

He had walked her to the car and then he had leaned over and pressed his lips to her cheek.

He hadn't meant to. It was just the side of her face, but still, he shouldn't have. Violet wasn't the girl he wanted. None of them were. Except Claire, Claire with her openness, like in spite of being hurt she would let you right into her eyes, right into where it was twinkling and jingling and spinning—merry-go-

141

rounds, windchimes, fireflies. That was where he wanted to go. But she wasn't ready for him, he had told himself—she's just a little girl, she needs time, and there was Violet, full of fury at him and love for the girl he loved, too. He kissed her.

The house was painted with red and white stripes like a giant circus tent. One of those atrocities that rich people build just because they can. But it was perfect for Claire. She wanted to step inside the most brutal of circuses so she could forget everything else. She wanted to be the fire swallower, searing away pain with flames, the disappearing act and the girl on the table who was about to be sliced up with knives.

She slipped in through the big spear-gate to the pool. It was surrounded by acres of lawn and lit with red lights so that the water looked like blood. People were making out, snorting coke and gulping down booze, sitting or floating in the water.

Then Claire saw the pig. It was live and fat but

small and it was running on its little sharp trotters with a look of terror smeared across its snouty face. No wonder. A man in a blood-spattered apron was chasing it, screaming, "Dinner, come back here!"

Dinner? she thought. Its name was Dinner? She reached down and caught the wriggly pig in her arms just as it passed by. Then she started to run. A man in the bloody jacuzzi reached out and tried to grab the hem of her dress.

"Hey, lose that friend of yours and come on in!"

Barbecue Man fell into the water with an elephantine splash, and Pig and Claire got away. But then Pig did a shimmy-squirm in her arms and he was so well oiled that he slid right out. She saw Barbecue Man flailing around in the water, yelling at her, so she ran into the house.

The party was wilder than anything in Violet's script. There were men wearing stubby horns and coarse fur pants, like satyrs, dancing with topless girls. Pigs and chickens were running all over squealing and squawking, chased by bloodthirsty Suits and

Starlets. Claire just stood there thinking, maybe I died and went to hell.

The thought intensified when someone grabbed her shoulder and she turned around and saw the self-proclaimed king of the underworld himself, Flint Cassidy.

"Looking for something, kitty?" he asked.

She just stared at him and shrugged. The room seemed to be tilting like a carnival ride. All she could say was, "What are they doing to all those animals?"

"Don't freak out." He steered her from the room.

They were in a guest bedroom with mirrors everywhere. Flint knelt down on the mirrored floor and spilled a line of coke out.

"This will make you feel better."

When she hesitated he said, "Come on. You want to be able to tell your friends what a wild time you had, don't you?"

The king of hell is supposed to know the words to say to get you to do what he wants. The thought of Claire's "friends" and the wild time they had had

144

or were having was enough to get Claire to want to suck up cocaine with any part of her body that Flint suggested. She got down on the floor beside him, leaned over and held the straw to her nose. The coke shot up there like powdered ice, numbing and stunning. Little diamond snowflakes twinkling in her head. She heard Flint whisper, "Your skin is so perfect, like it's never been touched," and she felt his lips on her neck, but she was bolting with coke and so she wasn't afraid to push him away.

She headed down the hallway like a suckling pig running from a barbecue, but then she was in a little sitting room and people with depraved faces, all sunken eyes and bitter mouths, were sitting around a table listening to a woman dressed like a gypsy with a black cat perched on top of her head.

"I sense a restless spirit," said the woman. "Spirit, what do you want to tell us?"

There was a loud knocking sound and Claire jumped as if it were coming from inside her chest. The people around the table giggled nervously.

"What's it saying?" asked one.

The gypsy opened her eyes and turned her head toward the doorway where Claire was standing. But she wasn't looking at Claire, more through her. "This soul is suffering," she said. "It wishes to share the secret of its tragedy."

Claire started to back away and bumped into a tall man, his face hidden by shadows.

"I sense the energy of evil," the gypsy said. "Here, in this house."

Claire ran through a crowd of people who were simulating sex in the hallway, and out to a glassed-in sun porch where a tan, blond woman in a garter belt and black bra had her head tilted back and was meticulously sliding a sword down her throat. Claire winced. The woman's eyes were bloodshot and filled with tears and the veins in her neck were bulging out. Finally she removed the sword, trying to conceal the gag as she bowed behind her hair. Claire could feel her own esophagus ripple with disgust. Some people clapped.

Suddenly a man came up and grabbed the sword away from the woman. It was Barbecue Man. He pointed it at Claire.

"You took my Dinner!" shouted Barbecue.

Claire backed away.

"You'll have to take his place!"

He lurched toward her. The sword swallower wiped the tears from her glassy eyes.

"Off with her head!" She laughed.

They were all laughing. Claire heard it building and building like a wall of sound—pigs and gypsies and dead spirits and blood-spattered carnivores. Grunts, squeals, wails, knocks, groans, guffaws, wee-hee-hees!

She was shaking so much that when she bumped into the man in the hallway she couldn't tell at first that they had collided. He steadied her and looked into her eyes.

"Are you okay?" he asked. He sounded like a concerned father.

Then she recognized his almost metallic hair and leather-brown skin. It was Violet's boss, Richter.

"Can I take you home?"

And what was she saying yes to? The kind refined gentleman who would help her escape the freakfest of the party? Or the king freak of all who would help her escape much much more? Part of her felt comforted, part of her felt afraid. Part of Claire felt cradled by the fear.

He had a white sports car. The valet put Claire's bike on top and they sped off down the driveway. Inside the car smelled like deep luxury and there was cool air wafting and soft music. She leaned her head back against the seat and closed her eyes.

Violet got to the party just after the BMW had left. She'd been caught in traffic on the Strip and was ready to rip off her skin with anxiety by the time the Hummer pulled up in front of the red and white house. If anything happens to Claire . . . , she kept saying to herself. But she didn't have the end of the sentence. All she knew was that Richter was going to be at the party.

But, of course, she didn't see Richter or Claire when she arrived. She tripped over terrified hens and pigs as she moved deeper into the house. A satyr grabbed her and started dancing around, his face pointed and devilish in the red lights. She struggled to pull her wrists from his grip, but he held on tighter till her skin burned red as if his fingers were made of coarse rope.

Finally she got away. But the house was like a labyrinth, and she felt she was getting deeper and deeper toward nothing when she saw Flint Cassidy. He was surrounded by a bevy of beauties and he didn't notice her, even when she tried to touch his arm. The Beauties jostled her away. They had eyelashes like silver spiders and lips like overblown poison flowers.

"Flint!" Violet shouted.

He turned lazily to her, brushing black hair from coked eyes.

"Have you seen Claire?" she asked him.

Flint just stared blankly.

"I'm asking you something."

"I don't know what the fuck you're talking about," said Flint, stroking the powder-white cheek of one of the Beauties.

"What about your agent? Where's Richter?"

"He left with some neurotic little blond chick. Probably took her to the office for an audition."

And Flint and the Beauties began to laugh hysterically like a pack of hyenas, braying, throwing back their heads, exposing their throats.

"Have you ever acted?" Richter asked as they headed down through the hills. The residential streets were quiet and empty as usual in L.A. at night. The mansions were ghosty white in the moonlight—mausoleums. There were no people in the windows, no life at all. Just dead cold beauty. The sky was a bruised purple.

"Not really," she said. "But you know Alice in *Innocent Ambition* is based on me."

"You're kidding? You mean you're the best friend?"

She nodded, but it was ironic. Not anymore.

Richter watched her out of the corner of his eye. "You know, we're still trying to cast that part. Who do you suggest?"

She told him her idea about the girl from *Kids.* He thought it was good.

"You'd make a good agent, Claire."

"I'd rather be an actress." She surprised herself by saying it. Maybe I'll get my boobs done and wear cleavage dresses and be featured in all the magazines, she thought. I'll date some hot up-and-coming actor and live in a big mansion and I won't have to think about Violet or Peter. I'll send my mother checks but I won't have to see her all the time and be reminded about what heartbreak can do to a girl who was pretentious enough to think she was winged, a poet.

"Not a poet like in the script?" Richter asked, as if he were reading her mind.

She told him how over that she was. How you couldn't make money that way.

"Do you have talent? As an actress."

She told him she did (she was being bold—the coke) and he said, "How about if you give me a little private audition?"

So Claire went with Mr. Richter to the office. The way he spoke to her, held the car door open and everything, felt like some kind of date. She wished Violet and Peter could have seen. She didn't care what Richter's motives were—it just felt like the only thing she could be doing right then. It was like walking on a tightrope. You can't stop and run backward or jump down. You just keep taking the little shaky steps while the crowd holds its breath beneath you and the stars laugh hysterically (but with a certain admiration) at your folly, through the peak of the circus tent.

They took the elevator up to the top floor. An eeriness, being there at night. The ghosts in modern places live in computers and fax machines, so it's harder to sense who they are, Claire thought. But there were ghosts. She could feel it. Hard, buzzing

152

ghosts with little blinking eyes and crushed dreams of screen triumphs.

Richter held the door to his office open for her and they went inside. He offered her water, soda, tea, coffee. They both had mineral water from his private bar, then he sat back with his legs crossed and his feet up on the desk and watched her like she was a little animal in a cage. There was a smirk on his mouth.

"Why don't we do this scene?" he said.

He handed Claire Violet's script. It was the scene where the agent kills the starlet in order to create something for the young screenwriter to write about. Claire started to read it to herself but Richter jumped right in.

"Now, think about it, this man is going to kill you. How do you feel? Your eye sockets. The place where your tongue attaches to your throat. Now try it again, honey."

"'Oh, please don't kill me, Jake. Please. I'll do anything.'"

"That's not good enough. You're not making me feel anything. It's a tough world out there. And I've got to be straight with you. You're pretty but you're not drop-dead, you know what I'm saying? So you've got to compensate in other areas."

"'Jake! Jake! Please don't! Oh my God! Jake!'"

"That's a little better. But just try to imagine that if you don't get this audition, that's the end. Back to waiting tables."

She felt a chill go up her spine and clench the nape of her neck. Something was changing in the room and she didn't want to look up at Richter. The crowd beneath her tightrope opened their mouths like hundreds of ghouls, replicas of the one in Munch's screaming painting.

"Oh God," Claire said.

Just then the door burst open.

Violet was a warrior. She was the wrath of death. Her hair was knotted up on top of her head and her body was pumped with adrenaline. Her eyes flashed hard at Richter, her pupils narrow as the blades of knives. Her small hands seemed dangerous, suddenly, the fingers kneading air.

Maybe the thing she had written had become real. Megalomania, maybe, but part of her believed it then—that her words had that kind of power. Power to hurt what she loved the most. After all, real life had never seemed as real to Violet as her art. Until now.

Claire had never seen Violet that way before. She looked, simply, as if she would die for her friend. And that was actually what Violet was thinking, standing there in the doorway of the penthouse office overlooking the seething city. She would have died for Claire in a movie and she would have died for her in real life, although neither of them knew exactly what the difference was at that moment. Claire was the symbol of kindness and innocence to Violet then. But she was also much more than that. She is Claire, Violet thought. And she remembered how Claire had shrugged that first day, revealing the wings on her back, surprised that wings and telling people she believed she was part of an ancient lost race would make her vulnerable; Violet remembered how Claire had supported her perverse crush on Flint Cassidy and squealed about it as if it were she, Claire, whom he had made love to. How Claire looked in the desert, dripping stars chasing butterflies, kicking up hot mica-sparked winds, transformed into the faerie being she always knew she was. How Claire had come to Violet crying, just that night (could it be? It seemed like forever ago) and how Violet had held her and how bony and frail she had felt, like a crushed bird and how all Violet had wanted to do was repair everything but it had gotten so much worse. And now, here they were, in a room in life or in a room in her movie, she was hardly sure which, only that the ending would have to be the way she wanted it.

Richter saw her, looked at Claire. He was standing behind his desk and his sleeves were rolled up and his tie was loosened. He just stood there, for a moment, without any expression on his hard handsome face, and then he started to laugh. He laughed and laughed, almost silently at first, and then it got higher and higher, into a kind of obscene shriek, and then he just walked out, walked past them, and into the hallway, still laughing. And neither girl moved, they couldn't move, they just looked at each other until they heard the elevator and the sound of the laughter was sucked down the elevator shaft and then Violet went to hug Claire, but she pushed her away.

"I'm so sorry," Violet said, trying not to let the waves of regret and relief in her chest explode into sobs.

Claire looked at Violet's mouth, twisted and holding in the sobs. "Get away from me," she said.

And then she ran out of the office and down the twenty flights of stairs to the parking garage. Richter's car was gone and so was her bike, so she went out of the garage and started to walk down Sunset with her thumb out. She heard someone honking and turned to see the Hummer.

157

"Come on," Violet said. "I'm not leaving you here. You don't have to talk to me. I'll just drop you off."

Claire stopped walking and looked at her. "So you can go home and fuck Brookman?"

Violet wanted to tell her it wasn't what she thought, that she had gone to him because she was angry at what he'd done.

"Claire. I love you. Nothing happened." It was all she could manage; her voice sounded choked.

A car sped past them and pulled up at the curb. The driver, a middle-aged man with greasy, scraggly hair in a ponytail, leaned from the window, checking Claire out.

"She has a ride," Violet told him, hard, like when she was talking to Flint at the party.

Claire could feel herself weakening, crashing. It was the feeling she got when she thought of her father, wanting to disappear into someone else, but someone who wasn't even really there.

"Get in the car, Tinker Bell," Violet pleaded.

She pushed the passenger door open for her, but Claire crawled into the backseat and collapsed, not looking up.

"Please," Violet begged. "It was nothing. Please tell me what I can do. Tell me what you want."

Before Claire got out of the car she turned and stared into Violet's eyes. For a moment it was as if they had exchanged souls, Violet thought. Claire looked hard and older. Violet felt weak with relief, like a baby. Too weak, though, like she couldn't function. Like she'd never write another script again. Who was innocence and who was ambition now, Violet wondered. She remembered Claire winged, holes in the toes of her shoes, making a faerie wand out of paper and glitter. Maybe there had really been a kind of murder that night, Violet thought.

"Conflict. I want conflict. Conflict sells," Claire said, slamming the car door.

She couldn't go to school. Maybe she'd take the high school equivalency later and enroll at a local college, get a job at a bookstore. But now all she knew was that she couldn't go to school and she couldn't stay at home with her mom. Her mom in the next room, wearing soiled sox, shuffling through the same scrapbooks with the pictures of a headless man holding her hand. Her mom who couldn't protect Claire from the faeries or from the real world. Claire could almost feel herself getting bigger each moment, as if she might burst through the house, her arms flailing out the windows, her neck up the chimney, her head popping above the rooftop. Swelling with pain until she burst. And at the same time she was shrinking, could feel all her bones when she hugged herself. She knew she had to leave. And there was nowhere to go. Not even to the one person she had believed would protect her.

I need air, Claire thought. I need desert.

When she packed her suitcase a photo-booth picture of Violet fell out. Claire started to rip it in half and trash it, but instead she hesitated. In a way she believed what Violet had told her, the night of the party and in notes and on her answering machine. Nothing had happened between Violet and Peter. But still she knew that something had changed. There was a relationship now between Violet and Peter that hadn't existed before. And the Claire Claire had become wasn't part of that. Something had shut down in her. She'd never be the Claire Peter had held in the fountain or the Claire Violet had held on the floor of her bedroom. Any part of her they had ever loved, even a little, felt demolished.

Claire put the picture into the bottom of her suitcase, but she knew she wouldn't call Violet. She knew she would leave.

The bus took her out of the city, under the arching cement highways, into the smog, past the demonic-looking faces on the billboards, past the car lots and malls and outlet stores. The dinosaurs seemed more sinister now—the one with the bigger head bared its teeth at her, and the windmills were frantic, hysterically whirring on the hills. In the distance a weird cloud bloomed—she realized it was a fire when she saw the planes flying back and forth with their red lights and smelled the charred air. Dust blew across the highway in a storm of pale howling grit and Claire wondered what she had seen in the desert before—it was like being on a planet of bone, she thought, a landscape of bone and pulverized bone.

But then Claire got to the high desert, and the Joshua trees. She wondered what they thought of all the tourists who came to look at them, not knowing quite why, except a famous rock band had come here, and it was a monument, yet there was some other reason the tourists couldn't explain, a strange stillness in the chest when they were near these tree-creatures that only chose to grow in very select regions; a recognition, like seeing some ancient ancestor. The sky flared like a bonfire of roses behind them and the air smelled of creosote—spicy, damp, fertile, although the landscape was so dry and barren.

The bus stopped at the entrance to the campground

and Claire walked along kicking dust with her sneakers. A bat flew past, near enough to make her shudder, but she liked it, too. She, too, would like to hang by her toes in the night, blissfully blind and folded in her own webbed black wings that could take her away when she needed them, take her as far as the full moon that had begun to rise.

For Violet the moon was only a disco ball, covered with mirrors and scattering rainbows. She was with Queen Esmeralda and Queen Matilda at the Red Cherry. The place was almost empty except for two beer-bellies shooting pool with a lavish yellow-sequinned trans. The air conditioning wasn't working and Violet's bare legs kept sticking to the red vinyl booth, so that it hurt when she shifted her weight— plucked skin. She wanted a stiff drink but had ordered a mineral water instead. In those moments of fear about Claire, she'd made a pact with the universe about her own sobriety and it seemed easy now when she remembered that night.

It was easy not to drink and even to avoid the coke, especially with the help of the chiropractor in the white turban and his liquid flowers, but it wasn't easy to do anything instead. She hadn't written in days. She'd refused every meeting and interview request. All she did was make phone calls to Claire and leave messages when the machine answered— which was every time. She'd gone over there, too, but no one came to the door. Peter had called Violet once, asking if she'd reached Claire—he hadn't been able to either. He'd invited Violet out for coffee and she'd practically hung up on him. It felt like another betrayal for them to even speak on the phone. Finally, she had made herself go out.

"Where's your girlfriend?" Matilda asked. She and Esmeralda had recognized Violet right away. They seemed, eerily, to know something had happened.

"We had a little falling out."

"How'd you make a sweet thing like that mad at you?" Esmeralda demanded, sucking on a cherry.

"I don't know. I fucked up."

"Grovel. Grovel. Grovel," Esmeralda instructed. "It's the only way. It's how Elvis retrieved me after a fling with a female impersonater named Elvira."

"I've been. She won't answer my calls."

Esmeralda grinned at Violet, teeth long and feral in her cocked, oddly shaped, wigged head. Maybe the lost faerie race Claire was always talking about would look like this, Violet thought. When Esmeralda took Violet's hands in her own furled ones, Violet thought, How beautiful you are, a movie star. On screen in the movie I want to make you will be the faerie queen. In our movie, she corrected herself, the one I make with Claire.

"You're two halves of a whole," Esmeralda whispered. "I knew it the first time I saw you."

That was when Violet thought of the desert.

The girl whom the boys thought was a fawn and tried to shoot, the girl who could fly when no one was looking, the girl with the wings on her skinny back and the child's mouth that was like too many flowers. That was who Violet was looking for.

But the girl had changed now, too. Just like I've changed, Violet thought.

On the way out to the desert she played Claire's favorite Tori Amos tape and thought about the movie she wanted to make. As she got farther from the city the smog in her head was clearing, her mind filling with explosive clouds in the shapes of adobe castles and flying girls.

"So you've abandoned Hollywood," she heard a reporter say. "What's the new indie piece going to be called?"

"Tinker Bell," said Violet out loud, knowing that there would be one and that it would be theirs, hers and Claire's. Our movie.

Claire on a rock in a shower of meteors. There were so many falling stars that she could hardly keep up with the potential wishes cascading down over her head. She kept trying not to wish for a girl with a mind like a miniature movie theater to come and find her, but she couldn't help it.

Finally, she closed her eyes and held her breath.

Violet, Claire wished. Claire wished, Violet.

She opened her eyes. The sky winked at her.

Just then she heard a car pulling into the campsite.

She got up and went to the edge of the rock. She looked down.

A dusty Mustang was parked below. A girl got out. Claire could hardly see her because of the huge bouquet of roses and lilies she was holding. Still, she recognized her.

Violet looked up as if Claire had called to her and they stood there like that in a meteor shower, in a silvery wind, in a spell of flowers, neither of them moving, and then Violet tossed the bouquet upward. Claire hesitated for a second and in the last moment she reached out for the flowers and caught them like a girl at wedding and pressed them to her chest.

If Claire had wings she might have flown away then. She might have flown off on rapid, cutting wings to faerieland where no one could break her heart because it was made of ice and could melt only into nothing.

If Violet had been in a movie she might have been fearless, safe in a knowledge of happy endings or even violent ones, neither of which, she knew, were real.

This was not a faerie tale. This was not the movies. This was life. It hurt more. It was excruciating. It was excruciatingly beautiful.

Claire could not fly away into the ice-white light of faerie. And Violet could not hide in the dark movie theater where everything could happen and none of it meant anything, finally.

Claire could step to the edge of the rock and climb down.

Violet could hold out her arms, reach up and catch her friend's wingless body.

Two girls, blending themselves together like a magic potion, and then separating, one more powerful and one more gentle after the alchemy, neither afraid anymore.